They Came On Doomsday

And other spellbinding stories

In 2030, the war between Good and Evil finally breaks out. Unexpectedly, brave warriors travel down to Earth from a distant galaxy to save mankind. Next, Judgment Day takes place and evil people are put on trial.

THEY CAME ON DOOMSDAY

First edition. August 14, 2023.

Copyright © 2023 Carlos Benito Camacho and Carlos B. Camacho.

ISBN: 979-8223756972

Written by Carlos Benito Camacho and Carlos B. Camacho.

Author: Carlos B. Camacho

Chapter I

Julius Hoffmann lived in a small town near Leipzig, Germany. It was exactly one O'clock in the afternoon on May 20, 2030, when he first noticed it; that dark spot in his house backyard. It was unusually warm for that time of year. He had taken a break from his work as a welder in his home workshop and was eating lunch outside in the shade of a mulberry tree when he suddenly realized that there was something wrong with the early afternoon sunlight.

In the middle of the backyard, there was a strange, black circular blot where there had to be sunlight. At the beginning, he thought it might be a tiny passing cloud, casting its shadow down to earth. However, not only was it perfectly round, but it was much darker than ordinary shadow as it steadily floated on the lawn. Had it been projected by a low-flying passing cloud, it would have shifted and changed in shape. Not only did that black disk lie steadily on the ground but it also seemed to stir the air around it in a whirlwind-like fashion. The grass and flowers lying inside and immediately around it waved from side to side, while the rest of the garden plants and the mulberry tree branches were static.

When he first saw it, the black spot measured about three and half feet in diameter. Looking at the big square garden from the stool he was sitting on, he had first noticed that one of the rose bushes, with its three red roses and a rose bud, did not get the strong summer sunlight as they had been overwhelmed by a round and extremely dark shadow. Then he looked more intently at it and became aware that more than a round shade, it looked like a weird black mole. He also noticed how the rose bush and the grass around it swayed from side to side.

The black spot seemed to be projected down onto the lawn by some mysterious object hovering high above in heavens. Julius looked up into the sky as he munched on a chunk of meat he had just cut off the fatty steak that lay in the plate nestling in his lap. As he could not see anything from where he was, he rose from the stool, put the plate with the steak on top of it, and walked to the middle of the backyard. Shielding his eyes with his hand, he squinted into the glaring sun for a short while, but he could not see anything as he only managed to get blinded by the strong light from the small solar star.

He went into the workshop, which was beside his house, picked up the welding helmet, and walked back into the backyard. He put it on and looked up into the sun again. But he could not see anything at all in the air in the direction of the sun, whose surface looked normal without the aid of a telescope.

The following day, at around eleven in the morning, as he had just finished welding a loose piece of pipe to a motorcycle frame, he looked into the backyard from his workshop. The sunshine was already splashing on the garden, but the spot of shade was not there. However, at 12:30 PM, as he took a break for a cool drink, he saw how the dark, round spot began to slowly appear. The first thing he perceived was the sliver of a black circle, like a black crescent moon, which grew gradually and steadily as the sun climbed past the zenith above. In a matter of ten minutes, the dark spot of shade had fully grown back on, but this time it was almost twice as large as it had been the day before. It had nearly doubled in diameter, spanning two rose bushes instead of one.

Driven by curiosity, and awed by this strange phenomenon, he grabbed his cell phone and sent a whatsapp message to his nephew who studied astrophysics at the Max Planck Institute at Leipzig University.

"Can you tell me what you exactly see, Uncle Julius?" said Klaus, who called him back right after he had read the message.

"Like I told you, I see a dark spot in my backyard. It looks much darker than the shadows cast by plants and trees. It's as dark as tar and it has grown considerably in size since yesterday. It begins to show up at around noon. I looked at the sun with my welding helmet but I couldn't see anything at all out of the ordinary up there in the sky. So, my question is what the hell is throwing that weird round shadow down on earth?" Julius said.

"A welding helmet isn't much help to find that out. It only prevents you from getting dazzled but you don't see a long way off. You need a telescope with sun filters, you know. I'll go over there tomorrow at eleven thirty," his nephew said, as he ate a doughnut; in contrast to Uncle Julius, who was lean, he was overweight like most of the young people in the 21st century.

The next day Klaus drove over to his Uncle's with his girlfriend. Julius helped him unload the long, cannon-like telescope and the heavy tripod from the pick-up truck. It was a high-quality professional optical instrument, which they set up in the middle of the round spot, which had grown significantly bigger, not only covering the whole backyard, but this time overlapping his neighbor's.

Klaus sat on the low stool he brought along with him and began twirling a fat knob to adjust the azimuth and point the telescope barrel in the direction of the subject to be observed. Then he set his eye on the eyepiece as he turned the small, focusing wheel to zoom in on whatever object was up there in the sky projecting the round, unusually dark shadow onto the surface of the Earth, on that tiny patch of land that was Julius's property. Ten minutes went by and the astrophysics student could not still find the object.

"Hey guys, what about a beer? It's getting too hot," Sophie, Klaus's girlfriend said, as she munched on French fries.

"I'd like a coke," Klaus said, turning the zooming wheel to refocus the telescope lenses on a region of space that was much closer to Earth than the one he had just been watching.

As Julius and Sophie came back into the backyard, bringing lunch and drinks, Klaus suddenly raised his hand to call his uncle's attention as he hunched over the eyepiece, intently looking out into space. Finally, his attention had just come across a tiny dot that seemed to float steadily in space in one place, on the outer edge of the Earth atmosphere.

"I found it!" Klaus said, loud.

"You did?" Julius said.

"Yes, it's up there. It's not out there in deep space but much closer than I'd thought it would be," he said.

"Do you know where it's exactly located?" his uncle said, even though he did not know much about astronomy.

"It's exactly at a point where you get off the pull of the Earth's gravity. It's weird, because it doesn't seem to move at all, neither from side to side nor up and down. It doesn't even tremble. It's just there, eerily steady, like a tiny dark disk, fixed in space, hovering on the edge of gravity boundary," Klaus said.

"Wow! Do you reckon it could be an UFO?" Julius said.

"Yes, it is an UFO, as a matter of fact, because it's a floating object that cannot be identified. Wait a minute! I think it does move, after all, but not from side to side or up and down in relation to a fixed position on the surface of the planet. I think it rotates in unison with the Earth rotatory movement around its axis. That's why it looks as if it didn't move at all, and this is the reason for the round spot to show up at noon every day at the same place in space, in this backyard, and then it disappears once the hovering object has gone out of alignment between the sun and the Earth. I don't know the reason for it to grow in diameter, though. What do you make of it, Sophie? What's your hunch?" Klaus asked.

As Klaus stood up and stepped aside, Sophie sat on the low stool and stooped over the telescope eyepiece to take a look at that mysterious object. She was also an astrophysics student but she was one year behind Klaus.

"It's so dark; darker than tar. More than a flat disk, it looks like a pitch-black gaping hole to me, like the entrance to a tunnel, but instead of being a mountain tunnel, it's a tunnel that opens up into outer space.

What if it doesn't move at all; I mean what if it doesn't rotate in unison with the Earth. I'm not quite sure, but I think that tunnel opens up at exactly the same time every day as it aims at a particular place on the surface of our planet, pointing or maybe aligning itself with a particular galaxy," Sophie said.

"Yeah, maybe you're right. But we don't know for sure. We're only certain that it's definitely not a piece of space junk that got off loose from some old, orbiting satellite. Because it's perfectly round and extremely black and grows in diameter every day. Anyway, I'll check with professor Lichtmacher tomorrow at the university. He's got a lot of experience and he'll use a more powerful telescope," Klaus said.

The next day, Klaus told professor Lichtmacher about the dark spot in his uncle's backyard and the weird object that projected it onto the Earth. At noon, using the university telescope, Lichtmacher found the object hovering unwaveringly in the same position it was the day before when Klaus saw it for the first time.

It was completely flat, black, and round, looking like a tiny mole on the bright surface of the Sun. It was not in the center but near the edge of the solar star circle and it could only be seen the moment it got somewhat aligned between the Sun and the Earth.

The Max Planck institute's professor agreed with Sophie's sharp observation that it could be the entrance into a wormhole, and it was always projecting a long beam of shadow in the same direction onto the same piece of land on the planet as it opened up when the junction of the 13 degree East meridian and the 51 degree North latitude lines got aligned with a faraway galaxy. This alignment imaginary line also projected deep into space, going by slightly off the Sun circumference edge.

During his long professional career, it was the first time professor Lichtmacher observed such a strange dark object floating so close to Earth. Despite his expertise and knowledge in the field of astronomy and physics, he was puzzled and astounded. Although Sophie's theory was interesting, he did not know what to make of it for certain as he checked it with his colleagues, who included American astronomers.

After a few phone calls and video conferences, it was a matter of hours when the news about that weird space entity spread like wild fire throughout every university and college both in Germany and the United States of America, eventually making it to the mass media as the first Earth tremors could be felt by people all over the world and picked up by seismographs in every country every other five hour.

The world scientific community was flabbergasted. In the United States, the NASA astronomers pointed their new, powerful orbiting telescope at the uncanny object but they could only observe an intensely black mole; so black and dense that it looked as if it were something hollow, like a well dug deep into space, like the entrance into a murky tunnel.

Six days later, the dark round spot had grown several times, covering four blocks of houses and half of the local park, practically the whole neighborhood where Julius lived. Correspondents from every TV channel in Europe and the United States were already at the scene, or should it better be said, within that mysterious circle of shadow, reporting about that unfathomable object that steadily floated out there in space in one place, slightly off the outer edge of the Earth atmosphere.

One of the journalists announced live that the world's scientific community had agreed that the growing black disk in space was in fact a small, black hole which had suddenly popped up in the sky out of nowhere as a tiny yet extremely dense point in the heavens. He went on to say that it opened up when an intersection of a meridian and latitude lines in the Earth surface got aligned with some celestial body in a faraway galaxy, or should better be said, became the target of some far-flung extraterrestrial object. When it opened up, it swallowed some space debris from old satellites and space stations orbiting around the planet.

Nevertheless it did not happen what the scientists had predicted it would take place as astronomers and physicists became even more puzzled, not knowing the real nature of the phenomenon. Their optic and high-tech electronic instruments were not enough to figure out exactly what it was as many of them began to make statics noises, with monitor screens becoming fuzzy and radars getting jammed and useless. Confusion and uncertainty plagued their minds.

Two days later, the beam of shadow being projected onto Earth by the disk-like opening in heavens began to get even darker without further growing in diameter. It got so intensely dark that it seemed to have its own gravity as it could be seen from a long way off like a black cylinder plunging into the Earth atmosphere from outer space. Meanwhile, TV reporters and technicians present in the circle of the now extremely dense shadow started to hear a very low buzzing noise, which, at first, they shrugged it off as a simple case of tinnitus caused by stress and mental exhaustion; the kind of stress caused by anxiety about the unknown.

However, the strange buzzing noise grew in severity as window panes and glasses inside cupboards began to vibrate. The whir became so extremely intense that it came to a point people had to cover their ears with their hands. However, just as they knelt down and screwed up their faces in agony, the humming noise suddenly trailed off to a very distant, weird whistle that seemed to come from the black object in space. Then it stopped altogether and silence arose and pervaded the surface of the Earth.

About half an hour later, after that auditory experience had phased out, the city dwellers started to feel cardiac arrhythmia; their hearts beat much faster than usual, with their blood pressure dangerously rising; then the cardiac beating dropped to a very slow pace. This was followed by nausea as they retched and vomited.

Struck by fear, people began packing up and leaving the city of Leipzig. The inhabitants of the neighborhood that lay within the spot of shadow had already left the area several days before, except for Julius, who seemed to have taken an imperturbable yet curious attitude about the whole phenomenon, despite the fact he felt the same symptoms as the rest of the people. Meanwhile, the same uncanny phenomenon began to take place in the United States of America.

As soon as mass media spread the news of what was going on in Germany, the frequency of the black gate opening up in deep space increased threefold as it began to project more uncanny black spots on Earth. Therefore, another one arose in the backyard of Charles McGuire's home in Lexington, Kentucky, United States of America. Charles was a senior, a seventy-four year old war veteran and retired construction worker and grandfather of four grandchildren. Two days later yet another black mole would pop up in Africa in a family home backyard, and another one in Asia; soon there was one in every continent near large cities on the same latitude line in the northern hemisphere.

Upon hearing the news on TV and on online newspapers about all the black beams being projected to Earth, people panicked worldwide at the prospect of a cataclysmic event, with the small black holes growing up and eventually swallowing up the whole planet. They crowded supermarkets to frantically get food and water as hordes of youths looted all types of stores. To stop the plundering and the sudden surge of street crime, governments were forced to impose curfews and send out their national guards. Meanwhile, the black disks had just stopped growing as the earthquakes ended altogether. Although the strange whir that came from the sky had subsided in intensity, it could still be heard globally during the night hours.

Chapter II

Julius Hoffmann was a sixty nine year old man, a retired professional soccer player, a former world champion who still kept himself in incredible good shape, despite his age. He jogged and worked out three times a week. In sharp contrast with his sons, nephews and nieces, who gobbled up tons of carbohydrates, Julius still ate the old fashion food that consisted of fried eggs, bacon and ham for breakfast, and a steak and fish for lunch and dinner.

Daily work-out and saturated fat kept him lean and fit, even though it seemed a contradiction with what government advised and prescribed. Aside from physical exercises, he had two passions; motorcycles, which he repaired and assembled in his home workshop, and philosophy, which he read and wrote at night in his big black notebook he kept in a shelf cabinet among his collection of books on different fields of knowledge. The study of philosophy gave him a sharp and independent mind which could never be influenced by mass media.

His healthy lifestyle made him endure the great reset event that had been planned almost four decades before but had been set in motion in 2020. Of course, it had nothing to do with an internet or an electronic device reset. It had to do with the lives of human beings as millions of people had been killed, not by a real infectious disease but by the vaccines and the WHO's protocols.

Having refused to get vaccinated, he had lost his job as a soccer team coach for the local soccer club, while two of his brothers also got fired by the firms they worked for. Meanwhile, his fifty year old wife had died in the emergency ward eight years before. She suffered from diabetes. One day, when he was away out of town to supervise and work as an advisor for a high school soccer team, she had had a blood sugar spike and had gone to local hospital to have it lowered. Upon arrival, she had been told she had to take a PCR test first in order to have access to medical attention.

Having tested "positive" for that "infectious disease", she had been sent to the emergency ward where they had put her in induced comma with Midazolam and Fentanyl and then they had intubated her. The doctors had scared her into submission, convincing her she was seriously ill and that her lungs might collapse at any moment if she was not treated urgently. Thus, she had allowed nurses to put a central venous catheter in her neck. Then a dark wave of premonitory unconsciousness had come over her as the Midazolam flowed into her bloodstream. The black curtain of oblivion had come unfurled, and she had spiraled down into a deep tunnel of slumber, from which she would never wake up.

Rendesivir had provoked kidney failure, while intubation triggered bilateral bacterial pneumonia, and fifteen days of Fentanyl overdose caused her death from heart and respiratory failure. The mass media name of that innominable disease had been written on her death certificate. She had not even been given time to make a phone call. A security guard had grabbed her cell phone and put it in a locker before she had been rushed to the emergency ward.

When she had been put away, Julius received a call from the hospital telling him about the demise of his wife. He was dumbstruck. He could not believe it! Upon hearing the news, he had rushed back to his home town and gone straight to the hospital. There, they had told him to go to the city mortuary where a clerk had referred him to the funeral parlor.

"My name is Julius Hoffmann. I've come to identify and pick up the body of my wife Astrid Steiner," he had said, to the reception desk clerk, who was dressed in a black suit.

"Yes, there she is. You can take her remains now, if you so wish," the clerk had said, as he had checked his wife name on a long list he had on the desk.

"I'd like to hire your wake and burial service. We're catholic, you know," Julius had said.

" The traditional wake service has been canceled by the government. So, they ordered us to cremate every corpse to avoid infection," he had said.

"What?! You incinerated my wife??? You, son of a bitch!", Julius had said, grabbing the skinny and pale funeral clerk by his coat lapels.

"Take it easy, take it easy! For God's sake! Don't yell at me! It's not my fault. We have to obey orders! Otherwise we get fired! Don't you see what's going on?" the clerk had said, pleading for understanding, staring into Julius eyes.

"What's going on? Tell me?" he had asked.

"They're making a whole lot of money out of this fake pandemic. Not only are private hospitals being paid ten times more for each day of hospitalization for covid-19 patients, but they're also paid ten times more for endotracheal intubation and they're also paid for each covid-related death," the clerk had said.

"How do you know it?" Julius had inquired.

"My younger brother is a nurse. He used to work in the emergency ward in a hospital on Adenauer Street. When he realized a doctor he had never seen before was killing patients, he asked to be transferred to a clinical ward," he had said.

"This is mass murder, for Jesus' sake!" he had said.

"Yes, it is, man; and human organ trafficking, too. And do you know why they made it mandatory to cremate bodies?" the clerk had said.

"To avoid widespread contagion?" Julius had said.

"No, that's not the real reason. Corpses are incinerated to erase any physical and pathological evidence. You can't do an autopsy on ashes. Fire destroys everything, even every trace of your DNA. A lot of vaccinated people are dying, too, from blood clots, heart attacks, and stroke. Every evidence must be erased," he had said, looking intently into Julius' eye.

"Are you sure of what you're saying," Julius had inquired, astounded and appalled at the revelation.

"Yes, and next month vaccination is gonna be mandatory. Look man, this is a big and evil hoax. This funeral firm's and any other funeral company's workers visit every public and private hospital morgue in this country. They talk to relatives, nurses and to frustrated pathologists who aren't allow to perform even a quick ocular examination of the body to see that no organ is missing. Every cadaver comes out in a sealed rubber bag and is sent to the crematorium," he had said.

"My God! This is something out of a nightmare. Somebody has to do something, to investigate this horrendous crime. Tomorrow, I'll go to the local police precinct first, then to the local TV station," he had said, with bitter indignation.

"You'll be wasting your time, man. Mass media and the judicial power have been taken over by globalist elite billionaires. Germany is no longer an independent country. This is something that was planned in America by psychopaths from big pharma and the arms industry to make mountains of money, to take over entire countries and to enslave their population through fear mongering about a 'lethal virus' whose existence hasn't been proved yet," he had asserted; looking convinced of what he had just said.

"What the hell does the arms corporations have to do with all this?! Julius had asked.

"Don't you see? There will be a war soon. Russia, Belarus, Haiti, Tanzania, and other African countries have refused to lockdown their people and, above all, they've refused to import the American and British vaccines. Before being shot to death, the president of Haiti had stated that he didn't want his country to be part of a unipolar world run by the American and European elites. Don't you watch and listen to the real news from underground sources?" the clerk had said.

"Underground sources?" he had asked.

"You know, independent journalists on video platforms on internet, such as Rumble, Youtube, and Bitchute. They're the only ones who have interviewed real scientists, such Michael Levitt, Luc Montagnier, Nobel-prize winners, and Micheal Yeadon and Yudy Mikovits, and many others. And they all agree that this is not a pandemic but a plandemic!" he had said.

"I've read a whole lot about history, ancient, medieval and modern, and I can say for what you're telling me right now, this is the most evil political agenda in the history of mankind," he had said.

That afternoon, Julius Hoffmann had picked up the urn containing the ashes of his wife and taken it to the catholic cemetery. There, he had set it in his family mausoleum, accompanied by his sons, brothers and sisters-in-law. It had been a very sad and poignant event in his life. He felt as heavy-hearted as when his mother had passed away some ten years before. However, the following day, he had begun doing research, trying to get objective and real information.

He began by watching videos in which journalists interviewed Kary Mullis, the 1993 Nobel-Prize winner, who invented the polymerase chain reaction (PCR) test to diagnose AIDS on patients. In three interviews he had stated that the PCR kit should never be used for daily clinical practice because of all the false positives it might give since the swab sample content was amplified at 18 cycles.

Julius had learned that the PCR kits being used in Germany in 2021 amplified the DNA material sample to 48 cycles. Thus, most of those patients who had tested positive were false-positive patients as a matter of fact. In other words, they did not have covid-19 but probably the flu or a winter cold. This meant those kits detected the patient's own genetic material, marking it as if it were the 'deadly virus'.

Along with his brothers and friends, he had organized massive public demonstrations against the vaccine mandates as he strove for the reinstatement of their civil liberties and human rights which were being blatantly violated by governments in Europe and world-wide in the West. During one of those protest marches, he had been arrested by the police and sentenced to spend three months in prison.

During the time had spent in jail, he had kept reading and looking for information from every source, both philosophical and journalistic. He had read George Orwell's Nineteen Eighty Four novel; a futuristic literary work which described the future of mankind, with people being slave to a centralized tyrannic world government funded by central banks. He had also read Noam Chomsky's Hegemony or Survival, and Erich Fromm's to Have or to Be. Meanwhile, he had been contacted and interviewed by youtubers from every political spectrum, one of them was very famous and befriended Ron DeSantis, former Florida governor.

The youtuber had told him that DeSantis had obtained important information that had been leaked through his Florida's Senator in Washington DC. It had to do with autonomous artificial intelligence which would be installed in armed drones and other flying machines, and anthropomorphic robots. These flying autonomous units would be fitted with a satellite guidance system and a 'search and destroy' program linked to a memory data archive, which contained every detailed information about every citizen in the United States, Canada, and Europe. They were also secretly building hi-tech tanks driven and controlled by AI.

They would be part of the elite's plan to reduce the world population to 500 million from the 8.5 billion people living on planet Earth at that moment. This evil scheme was in accordance with the Georgia's stone monoliths writings, which stated that the ideal world's population should be below 500 million human beings. Known as the "Guidestones", nobody really knew who had set them up. When they began to attract public attention, people took pictures of them as souvenir when they stopped by in their cars, but no one had ever given real importance to what the writings said.

Erected in the 1980s, these monoliths had been dismissed as the work of some rich and eccentric environmentalist; some lunatic man who had no connection with power. However, a thorough research done, in 2012, by America Unearthed TV production team had come to the conclusion that those giant granite slabs had been the work of a secret and powerful organization known as the New World Order, which had been related to the Illuminati. When vaccination had become mandatory in 2021 and people had started to die from blood clot artery occlusion and heart attack by the millions world-wide, a group of patriotic citizens demolished them overnight using a 30-mm gun and armor-piercing rounds, which some US Army's Colonel had gotten from some arms depot. It had dawned on them that the New World Order take-over was a real conspiracy and not a theory. An evil conspiracy against mankind.

When Julius had been released from prison, he had gotten a Telegram message from a fellow country man from Hamburg. He had already contacted him before while he was in jail. He had told him that it was necessary to get armed because of the dark times lying ahead. New lockdowns would be imposed on the population by the central government and those who did not abide by the new mandatory rules would be put in concentration camps. To make people obey, crooked politicians would use their national armies.

They had thought they were going to fight against regular armies, made up of human beings. They had never dawned on them they would employ robots! Although they had heard about artificial intelligence and automaton machines, they had not realized that thousands upon thousands of them had already been built and they had been hidden from public view; confidential information.

Believing he would fight against ordinary paid soldiers, he had decided to get armed. Since it was illegal to buy guns in Germany, his friend from Hamburg had sent him World War II infantry weapons, which had been stored and kept in mint condition in secret arms depots in large private homes. He had received three 7.92-mm-caliber Mauser rifle, three MP 40 Schmeisser sub-machine guns, five Walther PP pistols, and about fifteen stick hand grenades. These weapons had been kept greased over, wrapped up in waxed Kraft paper, and stashed away in long tin boxes.

Meanwhile, on the other side of the Atlantic Ocean, in Kentucky, Charles McGuire had already gotten his own collection of weapons long before Julius had, for it had been legal to have guns in the United States of America until it had been forbidden a couple of years before. He belonged to one of several paramilitary groups, called the Patriots, who had been planning to fight for their constitutional rights as well as for the re-establishment of the sovereign republican state; a government of the people and for the people. But, to achieve their lofty goal, they had to get rid of the plutocracy first; the elite's billionaires who had illegally installed themselves in power, through lobbying (bribing), as a centralized form of world government.

That was how, by 2029, Julius Hoffmann, Charles McGuire, Vihaan Gahnti, and many others men and women around the world had gotten ready to fight for their freedom and the survival of mankind. Little did they know that, by then, the psychopathic billionaires were also ready to exterminate most of the world's population with their powerful killing machines guided by artificial intelligence. Those human beings who survived would be made slaves and guinea pigs of their pseudo-science.

However, the baffling outer space phenomena, which had begun to take place right then, had made the elite temporarily put off the setting in motion of the killing robotic machines. By then, they had manufactured all kinds of autonomous weapons by the hundreds of thousands; drones of all sizes and types, unmanned tanks and helicopters, and anthropomorphic robots and their transport armored vehicles, all of them parked in military bases and hidden from air view.

Chapter III

When the earth tremors and the ear-splitting metallic noise stopped altogether and everything seemed that it would go back to normal, the board of the world enterprises' directors of the Central Government made the decision to go ahead with their plans of "cleaning" the planet. As a result, on that same day, the armed automatons began to roll out of their hangars. Those which had been designed to fly took off into the sky; then the tanks and armored vehicles containing robots drove across open land, heading for big cities.

The latest generation of unmanned helicopters came out of big tunnels in the mountains, where they had been in store for the past four years. As they sprung out of their holes into the air, they flew in swarms of ten and twenty flying machines. Their design, silhouette, and paint made them resemble green locusts, which bristled with all kind of known and unknown weapons. Meanwhile, small drones equipped with flame throwers had just begun setting fire to crops and forests world-wide to deprive human beings of food and cause massive starvation.

Half and an hour after he had heard about the rumor of the monstrous helicopters and wildfires, Charles McGuire received a phone call from his base.

"Hi Captain. This is Jonathan Clarke from Regiment 14. The monstrous helicopters and the blaze are real!" a retired US Marine Major Sergeant said.

"Oh, my God! Have anybody been killed?" Charles asked.

"We don't know yet. A farmer in Colorado shot a video as they flew overhead. The folks over there say they're coming from the Rocky mountains and they're heading east," the caller said.

Meanwhile, Julius Hoffmann had already heard the rumors about the 'Heuschrecke' (grasshoppers) moving in swarms across the European skies. As he was about to get into his pick-up truck to drive over to his son Peter's house for an emergency meeting with his friends, the low-pitched whir in the sky intensified again. But this time instead of rising into the higher pitch of a tuning-fork-like metallic noise, the strange noise turned into a high key harmonic sound which clearly resembled trumpets being blown far away in the four corners of heavens.

Julius looked up the sky as if he searched for the source of the now beautiful sound, but it seemed to come from everywhere, or the four cardinal points of Earth. As he thoughtfully observed the sky, a blue beam of light unexpectedly streaked down to earth from the black disk in space, hitting at the center of his home backyard, at exactly the same place where the black spot had appeared for the first time. It traveled down to the ground at the speed of lightning but it was not an ordinary bolt of lightning. It was a beam of light, having exactly the same diameter as the original pitch-black mole; in other words, about three and a half feet wide.

He was on the street, standing beside his pick-up truck, when he saw the beam of blue lightning. Drawn by the gravity pull of overpowering curiosity and wonder, Julius immediately ran back into his house and then into his home backyard. He stood there in awe, gazing at the uncanny phenomenon. Mesmerized, he advanced a couple of steps closer to the beam of light. He heard a melodic alphorn-like sound when the earth under his feet began to shake.

He quickly grabbed his cell phone and called his nephew. He looked up at the sky with wide-opened eyes, waiting for him to answer his call. Meanwhile another bolt of extraterrestrial lightning hit the ground, then another. The weird blue ray struck his backyard intermittently every other thirty second, with a strong strontium smell.

"Klaus, blue lightning is striking my backyard at the exact point where I first saw the black spot a couple of weeks ago. And there's a funny smell in the air," he said. "It's not really lightning. It's like a beam of energy that comes down in a wavy pattern and is followed by a trumpet sound," he added.

"Yes, we can see it, too, from here. Get out of there. It could be dangerous. It could splash out atom particles," Klaus managed to say before the cell phone went dead on him.

"You mean radioactivity? Hello! Hello, Klaus! Are you still there?" Julius said, to no one. "Damned!"

At that moment all kind of communication had just gotten jammed and knocked out by artificial intelligence, which together with the automated weapons and satellites were linked in a different network system. However, people thought it was the black spot and the blue lightning phenomena that had interfered with the global communications.

To put an end to what it wrongly thought was a black hole in the sky, artificial intelligence commanded an unmanned submarine sailing in the northern Pacific Ocean to launch two nuclear ballistic missiles up into outer space. However, as they approached the unfathomable black disk in the sky, these nuclear weapons mysterious glanced off their target, tangentially heading out into deep space. They had been thrown off course by some unknown force emanating from the hovering black disk.

The frequency of the blue lightning streaking down to Earth increased from one in every other thirty second to one in every other two second. Then it became steady, unwavering. It also got much brighter, linking up the unidentified object in the sky with the Earth below. It remained like that for about three minutes, when, all of a sudden, there was a flash of blinding red light which traveled down through the shiny blue axis from the black round celestial gate in a fraction of a second. A red, nebula-like cloud arose around the beam of light. The celestial fog spread out in every direction, engulfing the neighbors homes first, then the whole block of houses.

Julius had rushed out into the street when the bolt of red lightning struck the earth in his backyard. But he would soon be wrapped up in the red fog that poured out of his home through doors and windows. He momentarily thought it could be poisonous as he held his breath, but after a short while he began to breathe again, apprehensively and slowly at first, then at a normal rate. Panting, he leaned against a tree in the sidewalk. More than a minute went by and he still felt all right.

It was 01:30 PM, yet it was already dark as the small town of Konenberg was in the dark round shadow of the black disk. The street was dimly lit by the light from the celestial beam and a few lamppost electrical bulbs. With the blue and red lightning steadily shining down on the ground, the wormhole's black gate remained open this time as the red mist rose up into the sky. It soon spread out through out the skies over Europe, the Mediterranean Sea, and Africa. The land outside the black mole looked like a cloudy day but everything had a strange light red hue about them.

Julius was alone on the street, for everybody had packed up and fled the shadow-haunted town several days before. The dogs that were left behind barked and howled wildly everywhere. Then the trumpets majestically sounded again from heavens, soothing the dogs, which stopped howling and began wagging their tail as they turned around in circle, looking up into the sky, sniffing at the air.

Julius craned his head around the tree trunk to take a glance at his home. Now the sound of trumpets seemed to come from his backyard. He felt the earth shake again under his feet, but lightly this time, vibrating. Then there was a sudden flash of white lightning, immediately followed by a rolling thunder that came down from the skies. When the rumble abated, there was complete silence; a dense silence that pervaded the heavens above and permeated everything around him.

He stared at his home workshop door. He was going to get into his truck but decided to stay there, spellbound by these supernatural circumstances. A premonition had just arisen from a corner of his mind that something or somebody would come out of there at any moment.

A celestial being had just been teletransported from the black gate in space down to his home backyard on Earth. It had traveled down with the blinding flash of energy, its body curled up in ball-like fashion. Then it slowly straightened up as it acquired a tall human form. Looking around, he headed for the street. It did not come out of the front door, as Julius had thought it would but rather it jumped over the workshop roof down onto the street.

This being was much taller than Julius, who was six-foot tall. Not only was that creature anthropomorphic in form, but it was also extremely handsome, from a neoclassical point of view, with a thin oblong face and straight nose. It also had a very slim athletic shape; he was so wiry that every muscle in his body stood out like a piece of live cord. It looked impressive. Since, it looked so human, perhaps it should be referred to as 'he' and not 'it'.

To Julius' eyes, he had blond hair and blue eyes, and a body so accurately proportionate that he looked like those Scandinavian or Greek gods of classical mythology. His sharp steady look betrayed a powerful and well-balanced mind. On his waist, he wore a wide belt, from which a sledgehammer hung; its shiny head seemed to have been made from an unknown type of metal and its haft was short and thick, so that it could be wielded with only one hand.

"Get out of here, you human! Or you'll get hurt! The others are coming!" he yelled.

"Who are you? Where have you come from?" Julius dared to ask, looking at him in awe.

"In ancient times the humans called me Thor in Northern Europe. They also called me Summanus in Italy. For the Christians and Muslims, I am Saint Michael, the Archangel of Lightning! Get out of the way!" he shouted, loud, with a thunderous voice.

As Julius moved backwards several steps, there was another flash of white lightning. When the succeeding thunder subsided, another powerful being came out onto the street. He did not jump over the workshop roof like the Archangel of Lightning had done but he crashed through it, wading through compact matter, tearing down the walls. He was as tall as Thor and carried a shield in one hand and a spear in the other.

"I'm Mars, the God of War. We're sneaking and squeezing into your world through the black, round gravitational gate that was opened up by Lucifer, the Archangel of Darkness. We have forestalled him, without him realizing it. We'll be waiting for him in Europe, America, and other continent when he comes back once again into this world," he said.

Meanwhile, the same phenomena occurred in America, in Charles McGuire's home backyard, with the bolts of blue and red lightning striking the black spot, followed by dazzling white lightning and the deafening thunder. There a female deity stepped onto the street through his torn garage.

"I'm Justitia, the goddess of Justice. They also call me Akonadi in Africa. We're here to fight the final battle against the forces of Evil led by the Prince of Darkness, the vain, eccentric tyrant who deluded humankind into believing that he is unique and that he has the attributes to do whatever he pleases, acting on pure and harmful whims, violating the laws of balance of the universe. I'll be his judge and I'll preside over the court that'll bring justice and restore the equilibrium of matter and antimatter," she said, steadily staring at him as she held a pair of scales in her hand.

"Who are you? Where do you come from," Charles inquired, totally mesmerized and dumbstruck by this sudden apparition.

"We are living entities from a far-away world. Don't you see? We're from outer space. We come from another galaxy, and from another dimension," she said.

"What do you mean by 'we'?" Charles asked, stammering, gawking at such sublime being.

"Other powerful beings are coming," she said.

With every flash of lightning, one by one the aliens popped up into this world and moved onto the street. They were all tall, thin, and wiry. One said he was Apollo, another one said he was Archangel Gabriel, and another introduced himself as Mercury. Then, a woman-like entity sprang up in his backyard, with a very bright lightning; she was extremely beautiful and she stated she was Minerva, the goddess of wisdom.

A total of seventeen Archangels and fifty five Guardian Angels, known as demigods or heroes in Ancient Rome, had traveled down to Earth through the black gate in space. They included those that appeared in Germany, Africa, and Asia. Then there was a lull in the lightning, and when McGuire thought no more thunderous apparitions would take place, he heard the trumpets once again. This time, they sounded louder and even more harmonious, a sign that yet another even more powerful being would emerge in his backyard.

The last teletransportation was preceded by such mighty lightning that its blinding glow spread out in every direction, throughout heaven and Earth and through every living and non-living beings. It was followed by a deafening thunder that seemed to rumble on and on and on, without stopping. When it finally subsided, a tall and very handsome man emerged from the deep silence that succeeded the thunder. Then he walked in a solemnly and serene way onto the street.

This man-like being wore such a tranquil expression that anyone would have felt at ease, in peace, as he seemed to transmit a kind of subtle celestial energy which conveyed calmness and strength. Although he was not as tall as the Archangels, Charles McGuire had the gut impression by the countenance he wore that this outer space entity was much stronger than the ones that preceded him. He appeared simultaneously in Europe, Africa, and the Middle East as his presence was being witnessed by different people.

"Once again, I come to save mankind from the forces of Evil. More than two thousand years ago, you humans called me the Christ. I did my best but you were too primitive, and humans did not understand me; you didn't grasp what I really meant, and you had me crucified. But you only killed the body, but not the true being," he said.

"Are you 'Jesus'?" Charles' neighbor, who was standing beside him, asked, totally spellbound.

"Back then, in those days, I was 'Jesus'. Today, I'm simply the commander of the Archangels. But rest assure, for I'm still your savior who's come from a distant galaxy to save the human race and to preside over the Judgment Day," he said.

"From another galaxy? But you don't look alien to me. You look like mythological Greek gods, with human form," Charles said.

"We are far from being mythological, Charles. We're real, with a concrete ontological existence. We just take on the form of the ideal physical appearance of a human being you have in your mind. A black man sees me black; a white man sees me white," the chief of the Archangels said.

"What about the drones, the grasshoppers and robots that have begun to kill innocent people? They say the billionaires want to exterminate us," he said.

"Don't worry. They will be dealt with soon, before Lucifer comes back into this world. He opened this black gate himself. I knew he would do it, so I anticipated him and made our entrance surreptitiously. Had I opened my own celestial tunnel, he would have found out about my presence on this planet," he said.

The forces of Evil was headed by the Prince of Darkness and they included the deranged and psychopathic billionaires of the American and British elites. Also known as the Illuminati, they had already signed a contract with Satan long before during one of their secret meetings.

They were bound to drastically reduce the population of the Earth by annihilating 80% of mankind. The energy of each one of the murdered human being would be absorbed by Mephistopheles in his endless greed for absolute cosmic power, and the New World Order billionaires would own the entire planet.

In Germany, Julius looked back at the archangels and their commander from a short distance, with an open-mouthed expression on his face, not believing his eyes and ears. He was witnessing the most important and biggest event in the history of mankind and it involved powerful forces that had just come down from another world, popping up on the arena of human civilization. What he was seeing and hearing was the stuff of a science fiction movie and ancient polytheistic and monotheistic religions. However, it was real; it was happening there and then.

Since an early age, Julius had been brought up and imbued with Christian values and stories right out of the Bible, in a cultural environment of political and social stability. But now, all of a sudden, his world had just been turned upside down and he found himself in a state of bewilderment and confusion arising out of the current political events and strange phenomena taking place exactly at his home and neighborhood. But he had just recovered his poise and calmness through the presence of the chief of Archangels.

Drawn by curiosity, Julius slowly stepped forward, as if wanting to keep asking the gods a few more questions. However, he did not have enough time to keep asking questions, because right then Klaus and Sophie showed up in their car to pick him up and take him away from there.

"Get in! Get in! Uncle Julius, get in! We must leave this place immediately! We must go to an underground shelter!" Klaus shouted, as he pulled his car over to the curb.

"I told you to get out of here, you stubborn human!" Thor said, to Julius.

"What's going on here?" Sophie asked, in a state of confusion, leaning her head out of the car window.

"Ragnarok will finally take place very soon; a 'vitiosus proelium' (a vicious battle)," Dentatus said, in Latin, brandishing his gladius. He was a legendary Roman centurion turned demigod by Mars, who was also Tyr, or simply Archangel Raphael.

"Ragnarok! It's the end of the gods!" Klaus said, resting his hands on the steering wheel as he stuck his head out of the window to take a better and more careful look at those beings that had just come out of some parallel and distant world.

"It's the end of Evil and the unholy insane humans that rule this world," the commander of the Archangels, the Christ, said.

"This is the last warning. Get out of here and seek a safe refuge for you to be. Satan and his fifty beasts will soon make their entrance upon this planet from their dark, heavy-gravity world. This will be a very dangerous place for you to be in," Mars said.

As soon as Julius got into the car, Klaus stepped on the accelerator and took off in search of shelter in the city of Leipzig. As they got away from his home, they saw the archangels, angels, and their chief nimbly run and spread out quickly in every direction. As he stared at a distant point in the direction of his home, Julius caught a glimpse of yellow lightning. It was another series of successive flashes and thunders that had just begun to occur there. This time, the entities that were traveling down to Earth and landing in his home backyard, were not celestial beings but horrible creatures; they were the minions of Lucifer.

Having driven for about forty five minutes, they left their car in a parking lot and then they immediately headed for the underground metro station. They climbed down the flights of stairs and disappeared from sight. It was the kind of place Julius' grandparents used to go during the Allied bombing raids in World War II. A huge crowd of people had already gathered there, with food and bottles of mineral water.

As they went down the metro station stairs, they heard a powerful blast; a bomb had gone off somewhere above, in the city. In fact, it was an air-to-surface missile fired by one AI drone flying over Leipzig. It exploded in midair several meters above the ground, sending out bomblets in every direction, hitting nearby buildings and tearing out huge holes in them as they blew up.

More missiles were fired by the flying killing automatons. However, this time they did not reach the city skyline. Powerful shafts of energy sent by one of the outer of space entities had intercepted them before they hit their targets. Hundreds of people were saved. They ran frantically, screaming at the top of their lungs, looking for shelter. Fire broke out of gas pipe, soon becoming blaze.

An squadron of apocalyptic locusts joined the drones as they flew in circle above in the reddish skies; robotic vultures of death. They fired missiles that struck office buildings and power station. The light went out and the metro stations were plunged into darkness. People used their cell phone to shine light on their way down. Some underground stations were so crowded, that they had to take the space on both sides of the track.

In the United States, the murderous artificial intelligence-controlled helicopters flew in zig-zag among skyscrapers in New York City as they opened fire on escaping people. The fleeing human beings fell over one another as they scrambled for shelter. In Canada, the locusts machine guns blasted away at a crowd attending a football game, spewing a rain of depleted uranium rounds.

It was then the celestial beings decided to put an end to the slaughter. Archangel Michael fired a bolt of lightning which forked out into several lesser beams that spread out throughout the red mist like a web of energy that covered the entire globe. Electromagnetic waves hit the drones, unmanned helicopters, and tanks, erasing their memory disks, making them blind. One by one the locusts, drones, tanks, and the robots were out of total control and they stopped firing their weapons and many of them fell out of the sky, crashing into the ground with a powerful explosion.

When the psychopaths realized that their autonomous machines had been rendered ineffective and destroyed, they ordered the air forces to scramble their strategic bombers and fighters. Soon, thousands of them were airborne. However, before they had a chance to drop their smart bombs, these aircraft were wiped out of the sky by the Archangels. Submarines were also crushed into smithereens by Archangel Jeremiel.

When the billionaires realized that their plans to conquer the entire planet had been thwarted, they tried to escape by hiding away in their dens in the mountains. However, they were spotted and apprehended by warrior Angels, who acted upon the Christ's command. Then they were locked away to be tried on Judgment Day, the day of the last trial. Thus, the Earth's central government had fallen to the forces of Good.

Chapter IV

Only four days had gone by since their arrival in this world, yet the Archangels and Angels had already wrecked all the killing cybernetic contraptions. They had simply wiped the locusts and drones out of the skies, knocking out tanks, smashing robots, putting them out of action. They had also erased artificial intelligence from computers, freeing the world wide web from any type of control; they had tweaked and fine-tuned all search engines, making them totally unbiased, objective, and impartial.

To safe mankind from self-destruction, they had also rendered all nuclear weapons dud and useless, destroying all military facilities around the world. Meanwhile they had caught every human psychopaths that controlled the fallen Central Government, taking them prisoners, locking them up under guard until legal trial. However, they still had to fight the final battle between Good and Evil as they surreptitiously waited for the arrival of Lucifer.

The fifty beastly demons were already on planet Earth. They had come ahead of their master, Satan, and they were waiting for him near the black round shadow cast by the dark gate hovering in space. Fifteen of them had arrived at McGuire home in Kentucky, fifteen at Julius', while the other twenty aliens were in Asia and Africa.

They were very tall and powerfully built. Physically, they were half human and half animal, looking like some genetic experiments that had gone awry. All of them had horns and elongated faces, with hollow gaunt cheeks and long canine teeth. However, each one of them had their own grotesque and horrible features. One had cloven hoofs for feet, just like his master; some had paws, others had legs and feet that resembled those of an ostrich. Two of them had a very long tail, which ended up in a barbed spike. One had a proboscis instead of a mouth, for sucking out blood and fluids. One was one-eyed, like an ogre, with a huge mouth, and two of them had large bat wings.

Twenty seven hours had gone by after the total defeat of the New World Order and their killing machines, when strange silence set in everywhere around the world. It was not the usual peaceful silence inherent in a quiet terrestrial landscape, but an oppressive and depressing type of silence, thick and stifling. Then it was ensued by a distant, deep 40-Hz hum, which seemed to grow in intensity until it sounded like the rumbling noise of a thousand cloven-hoofed beasts running wild.

"I feel very sad. I wonder what's going on out there," Sophie said, to Klaus.

"Me, too. It was so quiet and now this weird hum that's driving me crazy," Klaus said.

"I don't hear any explosions anymore but I feel as if something bad is coming. This whirring noise is unsettling," Sophie said. An old woman nearby nodded, assenting to what she had just stated.

"Yes, it's really depressing and we're full of uncertainty, but we must stay put, here, at least for a few more hours, until we're quite sure that it's safe to get out and see what's is going on," Julius said.

Suddenly, the earth shook. Then sheet lightning lit up the sky around the dark gate. This was immediately followed by a dark bolt of lightning, or electromagnetic radiation, which could not be seen. It hit the black spots on the ground in the four different locations around the world.

A long, deep throaty sound could be heard as plumes of black fog rose up from the sites and spread out across the reddish sky like a murky pall. It was the Prince of Darkness, the eighteenth Archangel who had fallen into the abyss of endless greed and threatened the balance and harmony of the universe.

He had just come to Earth to exterminate the human race, absorb their celestial energy, and establish a frontier outpost and a dark beacon in the Milky Way, marking off the boundary of his Evil Empire. He and his malevolent minions were quite unawares of the presence of the seventeen Archangels, fifty five Angels, and their commander, the Christ, whose real name was Astrum.

"My faithful warriors of obscurity, my dense creatures of death. It's so great to see you again. As gratitude for your loyalty, I'll feed you with the most exquisite meat in this galaxy, human flesh, and there's plenty of it for you all! You can't see the humans because they have hidden underground in their cellars, tunnels, and metro stations. They have even dug trenches and holes. They're so pathetic. Yes, these tender beings are very afraid. They're small but they're delicious! And they have good energy to suck out of them.

"You can't see them but you can sniff them. You can pick up their scent and adrenaline. They sweat, tremble, and whimper and cry. It's the end of the world for them all! Come on, my minions! Spread out across this little shitty planet and let the real feast begin! Get rid of all the old yeast, the yeast of love and truth! Let lies and hatred break loose! This time Astrum, their savior, is in a far-flung galaxy, on the other side of the universe!" said Lucifer, guffawing out loud.

To make their banquet more exciting, the Prince of Darkness started hurricanes, typhoons, tornadoes, and other calamities all across the planet. Meanwhile, his demons marched out fast to the four corners of the world in search of humans to eat them up and liberate their souls for Satan. The first people they detected were criminals in jail and deranged patients in asylums, who were not able to hide away underground.

They tore out holes in the tall walls as they made their way into prisons. They killed and mangled whoever inmate they came across, tearing off their limbs, eating their flesh, and sucking out their blood as they went. Some plowed into the small power plant of the penal facilities, absorbing their electromagnetic waves. They also barged into psychiatric hospital, ripping patients apart.

"I told you, I told you, I told you a thousand times they were real!" a paranoid schizophrenic man shouted to nobody, crouching in a corner, with his face buried in his hands and his eyes bulging out of their orbits.

The evil ogres searched every building in cities and towns as they looked for human beings. However, most of them were empty as the majority of people were already underground in shelters, or in home cellars. The humans the fiends found in cities were greedy people who hung onto their material wealth and did not want to lose their money, assets, and gold bullion they had stashed away over the years. They also caught and gobbled up looters and thieves that broke open automatic teller machines to steal money and jewelry from stores. It was if the demons could perceive bad greedy people from a long way off through a type of uncanny dark sense they possessed.

The souls of those who were caught and killed went straight into the maw of Satan. And the Devil's maw for human souls was the 13th Oven of Hell he had on his obscure, dense planet located one and half million light years away. This planet was made up of extremely heavy unknown metals and minerals; elements not registered on the periodic table. The gravitational pull of this murky sphere was even more powerful than that exerted by a pulsar. Thus, when the Prince of Darkness opened his maw, he, in fact, opened a tiny wormhole that sucked in the souls of terminated human beings, which ended up in the 13th Oven of Gehenna. However, he preferred the souls of good people, who had more celestial light, or energy, than the bad ones.

"Where are the good people?!" Mephistopheles said, shouting at his army of ogres. "Pour souls don't satiate me. Don't you see? They have little light! I know good people's souls are much harder to get, though. But this time their Savior and his regiment of stupid Archangels and shitty little Angels are faraway."

"How do you know they're far away," one of the hideous monsters asked, exhaling such a horrible breath that an old oak tree standing nearby wilted immediately.

"I gave them a bait. I stirred up trouble in a peripheral planetary system of the Whirlpool Galaxy and a war broke out. They're there, trying to safe their innocent little creatures," Lucifer said, guffawing, with raspy voice.

After they had devoured all the baddies, who clung to their riches in downtown bank safe deposit lockers and commercial buildings, the ghouls went uptown for the goodies who had hidden away in every nook and cranny under the earth. Since it was hard for monsters to detect them, they began to storm houses, totally destroying them one by one, in order to uncover them. However, they found no one in sight as everybody stayed in concealment.

In Lexington, Kentucky, Charles McGuire and his family and friends had also concealed themselves underground, but in the big basement of Our Lady of Mercy church.

"What's that horrible grating noise outside?" one of McGuire's daughters said.

"It sounds like wood being torn apart," Lisa, neighbor, said.

Another neighbor slowly climbed up the basement stairs to take a look. As he stuck his head out of the hatch door, he saw a big one-eyed ogre lumbering along, trampling on gardens and ripping roofs off of homes. By some sense other than its eye, the monster noticed the presence of a human being. As it turned its head, it saw the neighbor's head sticking out of the ground beside the church wall. Then the demon started to bear down on him.

"Our Master once said the humans have holes under their dwellings," the ogre said hoarsely, as it made for the church.

"He said 'cellar'! Let's tear off their floorboards!" said another demon, who was almost a mile away. They could communicate with one another from long terrestrial distances.

"My God, my God, it's coming, it's coming! It saw me!" Lisa said, crying out in fear.

"Get out of the way!" Charles McGuire said, going up the cellar stairs, carrying a 7.62-mm M134 Minigun, whose cartridge belt came out of a metal backpack hanging on his shoulders.

When McGuire climbed out of the basement onto the ground, the ghoul was about eighty yards away. As it closed in on him, a horrific roar tore out of its slimy throat. The powerful deep guttural noise shook and cracked every window pane and the glasses in cupboards broke. Women and children trembled and screamed in panic below.

When it was about forty yards away, McGuire opened fire. The hail of bullets stopped the ogre in its tracks but it did not fall. It kept flailing its long hairy arms in the air as it bellowed. Upon hearing the whir of machine gun fire, Sean Bellucci, a neighbor that lived nearby, came out of his home cellar carrying a 10-gauge semi-automatic shotgun and joined McGuire.

The machine gun fire and the shotgun slugs made the monster stagger and teeter, but it did not die. It only sat down as it was hammered backwards by the torrential rain of bullets and slugs and steel pellets. The rounds tore holes in its body but they soon closed up as if its body tissues repaired themselves almost instantly. As Charles and Sean ran out of ammunition, the ogre stood up and began to bear down on the two humans. Enraged, it roared even louder than before as it went.

Just as the ghoul was about to rip them apart with its long sharp claws, a spear-like lightning came down out of the blue, striking the monster, rendering it paralyzed. Then the blue beam surrounded the beast in a circle of energy, which became its prison.

"Don't worry. Everything is under control. I'm a Guardian Angel, also known as a 'Valkyrie" by the old Norwegians. This demon has been taken prisoner," she said, taking off, leaving the monster paralyzed in an energy cell.

All around the world, one by one the fiends were defeated and immobilized in a circle of lightning by Archangels and Angels. Demons could not be killed but they could be trapped and disabled. Only their Master, Lucifer, was still at large and could not yet be spotted. It was necessary to catch him so that the goddess Justitia (Archangel Ariel) could commence Doomsday, or the Day of Reckoning, during which the psychopathic human beings, members of the former Central Government, would be put on trial for genocide and crimes against humanity.

Satan was very ubiquitous. He popped up in one place and then he immediately disappeared to spring up in another, using spontaneous gravitational field tunnels he was able to open up. He wrecked havoc here, then there, on the other side of one ocean, causing suffering and much pain to humans he dared not to approach for they had already been marked as 'saints' by the Christ. However, the commander of the legion of Archangels knew this and he sent his celestial entities out to every corner of the Earth to try to ascertain where it would be his next move.

"Where are my demons?! I haven't heard from them in a long while! I need more souls! Why are these humans marked with the celestial light?! Who marked them?! What has happened?!" Lucifer said, out loud, somewhat ruffled. Celestial radiation had a weakening effect on the Master of the fifty beasts. Then there was silence as he stopped to think and assess the situation.

Mephistopheles turned his head from right to left, as if searching for something. He also rolled his eyes upwards and from side to side, shutting them tightly, straining his diabolic senses to locate his evil beasts, but he only felt a deep void, which was only interrupted by the murmur of the Earth's magnetic field waves that fluctuated overhead. Then, all of a sudden, the Prince of Darkness heard the deep throaty voice of Abaddon, the most powerful and the most faithful of all his fifty demons, coming from a distant place on Earth.

"Master! Master! It's me, Abaddon. We've got a nice gift for you. I'm quite sure you'll enjoy it very much," the beastly creature of Hell said, to Lucifer.

"It's great to hear from you. I knew you would never disappoint me. What is it you've got for me?" the King of Hell said.

"I'm in South America," the fiend said.

"I know where your voice is coming from, for Evil's sake!! Tell me what you've got for me straight away!!!" Satan yelled, impatiently. The lack of news had ruffled him up.

"I've got a crowded soccer stadium full of goody good people for you, all tender children, teenagers, women of all ages, and old wise, virtuous men. There are thousands upon thousands of them. We rounded them up a couple of human hours ago. They all look so innocent and naive, and they haven't been marked, yet. You could rape, twist, warp and brutalize their souls forevermore before putting them in the 13th Oven. You could even make monsters out of them. Hurry, hurry!" he said.

Having heard the excellent news, Lucifer, who was in Sweden, opened up a wormhole and disappeared out of the Scandinavian landscape. Little did he know that the voice he had just heard at the other end of the world was not his faithful vassal, Abaddon, the powerful demon with bat wings, but Loki, the trickster god, master of deceit, who was better known as Armaros, who had been watching and following Mephistopheles during all that time. Armaros was not really a fallen angel, but an infiltrated celestial being used to pick up information about the whereabouts of Evil creatures.

Precisely at the same time Satan came out of his wormhole in Argentina, he was sucked out of sight and into another gravitational tunnel, which was opened up by Astrum. This new wormhole ended up in Nuremberg, Germany, in an energy cage, where the Prince of Darkness were paralyzed and kept prisoner.

"All fifty demons and their Master, Lucifer, have just been caught and imprisoned. Along with their servile human vassals, the psychopathic billionaires, they would be tried in Nuremberg, Germany, for a large number of horrible crimes and devastation they committed," the Christ said.

Chapter V

With the imprisonment of the Prince of Darkness and his beastly followers, every natural phenomena, life and human activity had come back to normal. As the World Central Government had fallen, new elections were held in the United States of America, Canada, and European countries. The European Union and NATO were dissolved. Each nation on Earth became independent again from one another and the peoples recovered their own sovereign government in which they were genuinely represented.

Politicians began to work only for their peoples' interests, for progress, for life, and for peace. Laws were passed by which 'lobbying' became a serious crime, a treason against the people, as it was from then on considered a bribery case, or 'kickbacks'. They passed legislation to keep businessmen away from Congress' halls. Therefore, tyranny had ended in this world of the Milky Way. However, the trials for genocide and other crimes had not taken place yet. They were about to begin. Lucifer and the fifty demons would be the first to be tried.

The first of both trials would take place at a soccer stadium on July 14, 2030, as presidents, famous political leaders, and prestigious scientists had been invited to attend the judicial processes to get rid of Evil. It was expected that heavy sentences would be handed down on the criminals by the celestial Court.

"All rise. The Honorable Judge Justitia presiding," an Angel commanded, acting as a judicial assistant.

Since the Archangels, Angels, the Christ, and Him, the omnipotent Presence who watched from above, knew Lucifer and his minions very well, due to their long and extensive criminal backgrounds, the first trial against them lasted only a couple of terrestrial hours.

"I, the Judge of the Supreme Tribunal, sentence Lucifer, alias 'Satan', 'Prince of Darkness', 'Mephistopheles', 'The Devil', and alias 'The

Tempter', to one hundred billion eons prison term in crater Delta-Epsilon-666 of the 5th moon of the dark planet Rollium in the JADES-GS-z13-0 galaxy," she pronounced, solemnly, striking the justice gavel on her bench.

"You bitch! You bitch! And you, who are always prying and watching from above! I'm talking to you! You, the self-proclaimed God! One day you'll hear from me. Do you understand? I'll kick your ass out of Heaven!" Lucifer vociferated, enraged, looking up at the sky, full of pure hatred.

When the Tribunal gavel struck the bench, blue lightning arose instantaneously. It compressed and flattened the energy cage in which Satan was trapped. Then a wormhole gate opened up in the middle of the soccer field, simultaneously pulling in Lucifer, who vanished in mid air. The fifty demons were also sentenced to one hundred billion eons to spend in the same moon but in a different crater, also compressed into a tiny cube of dense energy, and expelled away to the dark side of the universe. The craters were sealed with a plug of Protactinium, which sapped Satan's strength, putting him into a very deem slumber.

"The Court is adjourned until next week, when we start the second trial, which is the due process of law against the psychopathic humans for crime against humanity," the Judge said, bringing down her gavel.

On July 23, 2030, Tuesday, the second trial began. The main defendants were Anthony Vauci, Bill Cates, Albert Bourlying, the former chairman of Pfiser, Stephane Bancell, George Zoros, Jacob Rothschilt, and many other businessmen and political leaders from the United States, United Kingdom, Israel, and France. Many of these billionaires were part of what was known as the elite, or Illuminatti, a secret organization to influence and manage governments through lobbying.

"Mrs. Georgiva, do you solemnly swear to tell the truth, the whole truth, and nothing but the truth?" The Tribunal assistant said.

"Yes, I do," the defendant said.

"Remember, that if you lie and commit perjury, you will immediately receive a 455,000-Volt lightning shock from that little gray cloud hanging above and you will be disintegrated. Justitia knows when someone lies and the cloud, too." said the Court clerk.

"Mrs. Georgiva, during your tenure of the IMF as manager director, why did you advice poor country governments to put their populations under lockdowns and import the Big Pharma vaccines in early 2020," Archangel Jeremiel, the prosecutor, inquired.

"To thwart the spreading of the disease and to contain the pandemic," Mrs Georgina said.

"What did you tell them the consequences would be if they did not comply with your request?" he asked.

"They would stop receiving stand-by loans and other financial assistance for their foreign debt and infrastructure projects," she said.

"Then you forced them to put their population under lockdowns by threatening them. That's extortion and blackmailing. Didn't you know they're independent countries and you shouldn't be meddling in their home health policies," the prosecutor stated.

"But we had to control the infectious disease," she said.

"The lockdown wasn't designed to stop any disease but to impoverish most countries in the world and then take over their weakened government. Archangel Uriel, can you tell the Tribunal what is the consequence of a prolonged mandatory lockdown?" the prosecutor said. Uriel was the Archangel of wisdom.

"By illegally holding people captive in their own home, they are unable to go to work, and if human beings cannot go to work they don't get paid and they're unable to buy food to feed their family. When this happens, children get undernourished and suffer from malnutrition, which means their amount of red blood cells, albumin, and essential amino acids drop sharply. It is called kwashiorkor, and when humans suffer from kwashiorkor their immune system gets severely weakened and they can die from any diseases as a result," he said.

"Then it means that a very long lockdown instead of saving people it actually kills people?" the prosecutor asked.

"Yes, that is certainly what happens when people are not allowed to go to work. They simply starve. It is similar when there are food shortages during time of war," Uriel said.

"Then it means that when people started contracting any kind of disease due to their weakened immune system, the W.H.O. and the pharmaceutical industry authorities put all the blame on covid-19 or on whatever new infectious disease the American Establishment has concocted so far?" the prosecutor said, half asserting and half inquiring.

"Yes, that's certainly the case," the Archangel said.

"Then, once concocted, or schemed, they make it break out through mass media, spreading it through massive bombardment of negative and fear mongering news, to install psychological and cultural patterns of fear and thinking in the minds of people to force poor country governments to import vaccines and follow their health policies so that Big Pharma billionaires make even more money and the American Deep State take over their governments," the prosecutor stated.

"The real cause of death of human beings and the rest of mammals is comorbidity, which is the physiological, inflammatory, and nutritional state in which a patient is found. And it is only pathological bacteria and fungi what actually finish off the patient, not a virus. A virus is only a cause of a clinical picture and symptoms. If you are strong, well fed, in good condition, it is very, very, very unlikely that you will ever die from a virus infection. And here comes the most important fact: a real pandemic goes hand in hand with famine, and famine has happened during time of war. In the Middle Ages, there were two famous pandemic, with two infectious diseases outbreak; the plague and smallpox, with the former taking place during the Hundred

Years War, and the latter during the War of the Roses in England. And the 1918 flu pandemic happened during World War I," he said.

"Yes, I see the picture, now. People die by the millions not because of a virus but because of hatred and greed, as it happens during time of war and when you actually want to reduce the population and destroy countries just to take over the entire planet! These psychopathic billionaires, Your Honor, they are no longer happy owning a tiny island in the middle of the ocean, they want it all. They want the whole world for themselves! In this regard, they remind me of Lucifer, the Prince of Darkness, with whom they signed a contract. It is greed, that bottomless slimy hole they have sunk in, that kills people," the prosecutor stated.

"Court reporter, have you written down everything that has been said so far?" Justitia asked.

"Yes, Your Honor, I have," he said.

"Objection, objection, Your Honor, a virus actually destroys tissues," the defense lawyer protested.

"What do you have to say about it?" the Judge asked.

"No, it doesn't. Since a virus is not a living entity, it hasn't physiological needs, such as phagocytosis, that is to say 'eating', hence, it does not secret toxins. Only bacteria and protozoans eat and secret harmful toxins as byproducts, which damage nearby tissues. In other words, viruses are not inflammatory agents. A virus is only protein fragments trapped in a glycoprotein envelope. Its origin is a cell. It appeared on Earth more than 1.5 billion years ago, after the emergence of cells, because a virus comes out of a cell as residue. It is the cell nucleus' leftover, which the Golgi apparatus wraps up in a glycoprotein capsule. A virus doesn't eat, it doesn't stalk and ambush cells; it doesn't even replicate on its own. It's only dead organic stuff," he said.

"Objection, Your Honor!" the defense said.

"Objection allowed," Justitia said.

"What about HIV and AIDS?" the defense lawyer argued.

"HIV? AIDS? That's another hoax carefully schemed and devised by the pharmaceutical industry. 99% of AIDS patients are really drug addicts who are severely malnourished, anemic, with very low albumin levels. They're scrawny humans, living wraiths, because of their lifestyle. They spend weeks under the effects of drugs and alcohol, without eating anything. Go to the streets of Philadelphia or San Francisco and you'll see for yourself," he said.

"The prosecution requires the presence of defendant Anthony Vauci," Archangel Jeremiel said.

"Anthony Vauci, step up to the stand," the Judge said.

"When was the so-called SARS-CoV-2 virus isolated?" the prosecutor inquired.

"It was never isolated. It was discovered," the defendant said.

"What did you say? I don't understand it. Isn't it the same thing. Isolating a virus is the same as discovering a virus as an etiological source of a disease," the prosecutor said.

"The American team of scientists discovered it at the end of 2019, after a three-month period of research in Wuhan, China," Anthony Vauci said.

"Have you ever seen it, Mr. Vauci?" he asked.

"No, I haven't, but many scientists have," he said.

"Who? Can you give me the name of the scientist who discovered and first seen it?" the prosecution asked.

"No, I forgot. It was more than ten years ago. We had to discover it, the source of covid-19 disease," he said.

"Wow! It is the first time in the history of human medicine that you, crooked people, first discovered the etiology of an unknown disease whose occurrence and outbreak had not yet taken place. Isn't that preposterous? Who do you take us for, Mr. Vauci? It was the first time in the history of science you first start looking for the cause of an event which had not taken place, yet. Tell me, how do you know there is a cause of a phenomenon if you haven't seen the occurrence, yet?" the prosecutor said.

"I...I...I...I don't know what you mean, Sir," Anthony Vauci stammered, with his Adam's apple moving up and down as he swallowed bitter saliva.

"In order to start looking for a cause, you first have to see, witness, and realize the concrete existence of an event. In other words, in order to begin searching for the etiological agent, you have to witness the concrete presence of a new clinical picture and symptoms, which indicate it is really a new disease," Archangel Jeremiel said.

"I guess so," Anthony Vauci said, looking blanking at some point in space, as if his soul had been sucked out of his body.

"It was only after poliomyelitis broke out, with its distinct symptoms and clinical picture, that scientists started looking for a cause, to know whether it was provoked by a bacterium or a virus. You cannot forecast neither the appearance of a new virus nor the outbreak of a new disease. You only discover the cause long after a new disease breaks out," he said.

"Yes, I guess you're right, Sir," the defendant said, in a very low voice that could hardly be heard.

"How come the pharmaceutical industry began producing the vaccine before the new "disease" broke out? Tell me, Mr Vauci," the prosecutor demanded. "Did you know, that Edward Jenner was able to produce an effective vaccine against smallpox only because the disease had broken out hundreds of years before and without ever seen a virus. He manufactured the vaccine only through careful observation of patients and their symptoms. He was a very honest and bright man who really cared for the health of human beings. He is a saint, you know," the prosecutor added.

"Mr. Vauci, you'd better tell the Court the truth. That gray cloud hanging over you has become bigger. It means you are not telling us the truth and you can get the 455,000-Volt shock at any moment and get carbonized," the Judge said. It was not a bluff, and it was necessary, because these billionaires were pathological liars.

"All right, OK, OK, OK. It was a hoax. I confess before the Tribunal. It was all a hoax, the biggest fraud in history. We invented it to impose an agenda and a vaccine to reduce the population. It was a fictional disease and a fictional virus. It was all made up. This new disease had the symptoms of all known and proven diseases. It was very convenient. Bill Cates substantially contributed to it, and he came along with this idea of spreading Legionella bacteria through air conditioning ducts in major hospitals, Bacillus anthracis bacteria, and Aedes aegypti mosquitoes in parks and countryside areas, using aircraft and drones so that people got sick and we made them believe it was covid," he said.

There was long and deep silence at the stadium after Anthony Vauci admitted that it was all a lie. It was as if everybody had just begun remembering their dear relatives, mothers, fathers, brothers and sisters who died during the hoax disease treatment or from heart attacks after they had been vaccinated.

"Tell me about the hoax disease treatment," the prosecutor demanded, with firm voice.

"We imposed the W.H.O.'s protocol treatment through financial extortion and bribing presidents and politicians. Also, private hospitals and doctors were paid ten times higher for each day of hospitalization and for the use of ventilators and Remdesivir on covid-19 patients. Thus, instead of treating bronchitis or asthma patients, they would rather treat 'covid-19 patients', because it was a whole lot more profitable for them. All they had to do was to write down the word 'covid-19' as diagnose on the clinical report sheet instead of 'flu' or 'bronchitis'. Thus, covid was only ink on paper," he said.

"But tell me what the W.H.O.'s treatment was all about," the Archangel asked.

"The goal of the W.H.O.'s protocol was to dramatize the disease, to make it look dangerous. Once a patient tested positive for covid, using the fraudulent PCR test kid, doctors had to tell him that he was seriously ill, to scare the shit out of him, even though he was wide awake, I mean, conscious, as he could walk and move and talk normally. Then he was sent to the emergency ward, where a doctor put him in medically-induced coma, using Midazolam or Fentanyl through central intravenous route. Once he was in deep coma, I mean dangerously in deep coma, the patient was intubated, with ventilator, because he was in such deep coma he was unable to breathe in his own. Then Remdesivir was administered. Intubation caused bacterial pneumonia, the anti-viral drug provoked kidney failure and the patient died, because of the treatment, but relatives were told that it was 'covid' that had killed him," he said.

"Do you know why I have been using 'Mr.' as a form of address instead of 'Dr.' all this time? Because you aren't a real Doctor. You are a fraud, a crook, a criminal," Archangel Jeremiel said.

Almost two weeks had gone by, with witnesses and scientists giving testimony as they sat on the court stand, when the Jury of Angels finally reached a verdict. Both prosecution and defense had argued tenaciously about the genocide cases. Thousands of people were sitting on the stadium stands, watching it all, talking to one another.

"Before putting an end to this legal process, Archangel Jophiel will proceed to make a final statement to enlighten the humans and make them aware again," Justitia said.

"Once upon a time, many thousand human years ago, Homo sapiens were bestowed upon by God with the light of reason, which is the most precious gift that He can ever confer on a living being.

"What is 'reason'? It is the light; the faculty to fully understand reality. But what does the word 'understand' mean? It means to be able to see clearly the differences between the parts that make up reality, and then be able to synthesize them into an understandable whole that makes sense to you. To reason means to see the cause of an event and the effect on the real world. And this capacity of analyzing all the pieces that make up your tangible circumstances enables you to choose, that is to say, to pick out what is best for you, the best option with which to achieve your goal.

"Thus, reason is to be able to choose what is right for you, and discard what is wrong and useless. And what is right for you is to choose the right way to do the things that will keep you and your beloved ones alive, healthy, in harmony, and in comfortable situations. In other words, 'reason' is to know to make the right choice to achieve your goals without hurting your fellow beings. And in most cases, to achieve your goals, you need your fellow beings and work together with them in unison, and for this you need a common language through which you make yourself understood.

"When I say that sometimes you need to work together with your fellow beings to accomplish your objective, I mean that you have to work as a team in a way that everybody that takes part in the enterprise gets a fair share. When they do not get a fair share as compensation for their time and work invested, then it means you are using and exploiting them. And this means that you are manipulating them, using the common language to induce in them behavior that is favorable for your selfish purpose. You exploit them, using lies and deceits.

"When this happens, it is because you are a psychopath and, as such, you lack integrity and empathy. And when you lack integrity, you are sick; you are warped, and you stop using 'reason' and start employing a disengaged and small part of you, and you become a dwarf, selfish being who schemes all the time to obtain things to fill that bottomless well, which is your greed.

"These psycopathic billionaires are selfish beings who believe they are the center of the universe and they have been using and exploiting human beings for many years. With the help of mass media, they created warped patterns of feeling and thinking tightly woven into an awry moral fabric that has sapped, weakened, and worn away the common people self-esteem and sense of worth, splitting the human mind and rendering Homo sapiens schizoid, fearful, and distrustful," Archangel Jophiel said, finishing her final statement.

"Members of the Jury, have you reached a verdict?" Justitia inquired.

"Yes, Your Honor," one of them said.

"Officer, please read the verdict," the Judge said.

"The Jury finds all sixty six accused guilty as charged," the Court officer read, loud.

The stadium roared with the people exclamation of surprise and awe. Then they cheered and applauded and laughed with joy.

"Jesus! It was about time!" a middle-aged man said.

"That's because you didn't have faith. The truth always goes afloat into view," his wife said.

"Bye bye, billionaires! Bye bye! Bye bye! Mankind don't need you, you crooked bastards!" a little girl shouted, loud.

"Order, order! Keep silent please. Now, Judge Justitia will hand down the sentence," the officer said.

"Using the power conferred upon me by the Almighty, I, Justitia, sentence all sixty six accused to the termination of their terrestrial life through a million-volt shock, and their dark souls to eternal residence in the 13th Oven of Hell," Justitia pronounced.

As soon the gavel hit the bench, lightning sprang up from the gray cloud and struck all sixty six guilty of genocide. They were immediately pulverized as plumes of smoke rose into the sky.

The Outbreak

Carlos B. Camacho

The Outbreak Carlos B. Camacho

It was March 19, 2020. I had just taken a shower when I sat down at the kitchen table to have dinner. As usual, I turned on the TV set to listen to the evening news. As I chewed a chunk of juicy steak, I listened to what the anchorman said. The viral infection seemed to be spreading throughout the whole world quite fast. Thus, it had purportedly become a pandemic. As a result, the president of Argentina had just put the whole country under quarantine to avoid the spread of the infectious disease.

The infectious disease was covid-19, which was allegedly caused by an apparent new virus called SARS Cov-2. According to the mass media, the covid-19 outbreak had begun in Wuhan, China, from which it had spread to Italy, Spain, France, and then to the United States. At the beginning, it all seemed very distant as I had never thought it would ever leap down to the southern hemisphere and disseminate throughout South America. I just tried to imagine what it would be like to be put on home lockdown as nation governments decided to quarantine whole cities and towns as well as the rural residents in the countryside area.

Although an infectious disease outbreak and its subsequent epidemic and pandemic propagation were not new to human beings, it was the first time in the history of mankind that entire healthy populations were put under house arrest and systematically bombarded by mass media with a campaign of information overload apparently designed to strike fear and anxiety in the heart and mind of the people rather than giving objective information about how to reinforce our immune system and take care of oneself.

In the past, even during the Middle Ages, when the science of medicine was virtually non-existent, it was the infected people who were quarantined, but never the healthy, asymptomatic ones. Thus, the 21st century governments approach to the pandemic was not logical as they all used exactly the same world-wide protocols, regardless of local customs, habits, and nutritional status. This fact, and not the disease, was eerie; as if there were some hidden global power hovering over civilization like an ominous black cloud. Everywhere in this world, governments were replacing their national Constitutions and laws with foreign rules written by wealthy businessmen.

"The quarantine is a mandatory lockdown of the whole population. You must stay indoors. Anyone not complying with the presidential confinement decree will be arrested and sent to a federal prison," the anchorman said.

"What about our constitutional rights? I have to go to work, for God's sake! We're not criminals!" I said to myself, as I intently watched the images of coffins set in a row in northern Italy on the TV screen.

Right then my girlfriend, who lived on the other side of the city, sent me a WhatsApp message, asking me if I had heard the news.

"It means we won't be able to meet for fifteen days. That's a long time," I answered her, realizing that my cell phone was running low on battery.

As I put my phone on its battery charger, I realized that the electricity socket had become loose and needed to be fixed. I kept the screwdrivers, pliers, wrenches, and other tools down below in the cellar. It had been a long time since I had last used them, and now I would have plenty of time to do all the repairing needed to be done around the house. I also kept my shotgun, pistol and hunting gear in the store room down below. So, I decided to go fetch all the stuff that I needed to fix all the broken things at home; things that had been left undone, such as changing the worn-out washer of the dripping faucet in the bathroom.

As I climbed down the cellar stairway, I could hear a public vehicle siren wailing as it drove by the front of the house. 'Perhaps it was an ambulance carrying the first infected man, or perhaps it was just a police car on its way to fight crime,' I thought.

The prospect of getting infected did not scare me at all, though, for I considered myself to be in good health and physical condition as I worked out at a local gym regularly and ate healthily; plenty of red meat, cattle liver, nuts, and plenty of non-starchy vegetables. I also did not drink alcohol, nor did I consume drugs. However, when I heard that siren, I got worried about my siblings and other relatives, especially about a brother who suffered from diabetes.

The house where I lived was a very old one-story building, with a colonial-style facade. The walls were thick. So, they muffled out all external noise. Because of its age, some of the wooden floorboards in the living room and bedrooms were rotten and loose. Also the cellar stairway steps were in the same bad condition. They creaked as I trod on them on my way down to the underground store room. The journalists' voices coming from the TV set died down as I went down below the ground level.

I was thinking that fifteen days were a hell of a long time to live without sex, when I trod on the sixth step. As I set my foot on it, with my full body weight on top, that wooden stair suddenly gave in and broke with a cracking noise. As I went down through the pieces of the broken board that made the step, my head hit the fifth one. As I landed on the cellar ground, my right foot stamped on one of the electrical wire spools that had been stored under the stairway a long time before. Suddenly I lost consciousness as my whole world blacked out.

A long while of dark unawareness went by when I finally woke up, moaning and squirming as I lay on the cold basement floor among wire spools and boxes containing my childhood toys. My head, back, and ankle hurt sharply as excruciating pain shot throughout my whole body in waves at the rhythm of my heartbeat. Also my side ached as I breathed. I must have hit a spool flange. I turned my head from side to side, looking around as I tried to pull myself together.

My whole life history ran on the screen of my mind as I tried to focus my awaken consciousness on my present circumstances. How had I ended up there on the cellar floor severely injured? I wondered. Yes, I remembered it now; the pandemic. However, I was well aware now that it was certainly not the virus but the government lockdown and, of course, the rotten wooden step that led me down to my abject underground circumstances. Being injured, I wondered how I would be able to climb up the stairs and get back into the kitchen, where my cell phone was, and call for help. I could barely move. I wondered how long I had been lying there unconsciously.

I craned my head one more time to look around, this time with a higher degree of awareness. I saw the family's old books on the shelves on the wall on the other side of the underground room; they were covered by a transparent plastic sheet. Below them, there were boxes piled up three high. They contained cans of food, old clothes, long play records, magazines, and old house appliances people no longer used. Right beside them, there were four old chairs standing in a line. On top of them, there were more books on medicine and an old six-band radio. To my relief, I also saw bottles of mineral water, which were standing on the floor against the other cellar wall. They were once stored there by my father a couple of years before he died; "in case of a civil war breaks out," he had once said. I was very thirsty and I felt my mouth extremely dry.

Suffering a lot of pain and with great difficulty, I managed to turn around to change position. Lying prone now, I began to crawl across the floor. I grimaced as I slowly inched forward. When I finally got there, I stretched out my hand and grabbed the nearest bottle. I felt the cool soothing water flowing down my gullet as I drank, with my chest slightly raised off the floor.

Having drunk half the water contained in the bottle, I breathed a long sigh of relief. As I lay there prone, I wondered what day of the week and what time it was. I had lost my bearings and the last things I remembered doing was watching the evening news and putting my cell phone on the charger; I also recalled that the socket was loose and I needed a screwdriver and some tools to do some repairing around the house.

I lifted my head, turning it sideways. I looked at the old radio and as I wondered if it still worked or if the batteries were still charged. I crawled again across the basement tiled floor. I extended my arm and took hold of it, setting it down on the floor. Fortunately, it had the wire and plug, which I inserted with great difficulty into the AC socket in the wall right above the baseboard. Then I twisted the radio 'on' knob clockwise. There was click and it came on alive.

"More than eighteen hundred people infected with coronavirus were hospitalized today in Tucuman. That makes more than fifty thousand patients suffering from covid-19 at the moment in Argentina. Most of them are kept in intensive care wards," said the announcer from a local AM radio station.

"Oh, my God! This is like the Plague back in the Middle Ages. May be worse," I said to myself, as I got extremely anguished, thinking of my brother and sisters. I also thought of my girlfriend, Virginia, who lived on the other side of town. "I hope she's still alive," I thought.

"The Minister of Public Health informed that fifteen thousand four hundred and fifty people have already died of covid-19 in the country. He also stated that the peak of the infection will be observed next month as he stressed the importance of social distance, advising the population to stay at home," the radio announcer said.

"My God! I wonder how the rest of the world is faring with it," I thought, remembering that I had a cousin living in northern Italy.

Tired of lying on my belly, I turned around with great exertion as I sat up, feeling an agonizing pain in my side. With my head and upper part of my body in the vertical position now, I was able to see more clearly and focus my attention on my circumstances and physical condition. I decided to do a body check-up to see how badly I had been injured in the fall.

First, I examined my legs; I could bend my knees, but I could not move my right foot, which hurt harrowingly. Although it had greatly swollen, there was no protrusion of any kind. I apparently had a non-displaced fracture of the fibula (calf bone) slightly above the lateral malleolus (ankle). Then I breathed in deeply; as I did so, I felt a sharp pain in my right side. With my left hand, I gingerly ran the tip of my fingers along my ribs. On the fourth and fifth ones, they sank a bit at a hollow spot; they were broken. Next I gently touched the back of my head and I felt a protruding sore bump, which was the size of a peach; it was not that serious in itself; it would have been alarming if I had gotten a subdural hematoma, which apparently was not the case.

Although I had bruises and scratches in other parts of my body, those were the three sore spots, from which pain radiated as if in waves. My head ached. Inadvertently, I breathed in deeply again, as if by reflex. Feeling the sharp pain in my side, I screwed up my eyes. Then I touched my T-shirt. It was thoroughly wet. It seemed I had sweated profusely, even though it was not hot. I must have had high fever during the time of unconsciousness. If it was a bacterial infection that had caused it, it seemed that my immune system had successfully overcome it.

I touched my face with my fingertips and I noticed that my eyes were sunken as my mouth still felt dry and sticky; that was a sign of severe dehydration. I raised the bottle and gulped down the rest of the water.

Aside from the pain, I felt weak. Hopefully, I would soon regain my strength and be able to go up the stairs and get out of there. The problem was the missing step. Each one of the steps had been set relatively high above one another. For the time being, I would not be able to either jump over the wide gap in the stairway on one leg or pull myself over it, with my hands hanging on to the next stair above, because of my broken rib.

As I turned off the radio, the cellar was plunged into thick silence. Only the muffled squeaking sounds of some mouse in the floor woodwork above could be heard.

"Help! Help! Help!" I shouted, in the hope somebody could hear me. Then I remembered the quarantine and that the streets were empty; empty of people.

Everybody was in their home, shut off from society, and my relatives would not be able to come over in fifteen days as I remembered the radio announcer repeatedly telling the people to stay at home and keep social distance, which sounded irrational to me.

I had been taught at the university that human beings, like the rest of the order Primates, are social creatures. Physical contact, especially mother-child skin contact, and watching the facial expressions of our beloved ones are of the utmost importance for the development of our personality. Man succeeded in his struggle for survival not alone but as a member of a social group, and the fact that we were able to communicate our feelings and thoughts to one another was an irrefutable proof. But now they were telling us to be isolated from one another and to erase our human face, with the sinister cloak of a mandatory mask.

Although I realized it was useless to call out for help, for no one would hear me, I hoped that I would get better and be able to rise on my feet and get out of that basement by myself. But now the fever still came back for about an hour and then ebbed away. I took off my T-shirt and wrapped it around my ankle, as tight as I could, so that the broken bone did not get displaced.

As I finished fixing my ankle, I heard the muffled and distant wailing of another ambulance going by. Then it faded away to give in to that sepulchral silence. I could only hear my stomach rumble. I was hungry. I did not know how long I had been without eating. I only knew I had lost weight as my abdomen had no fat reserve left at all. It was flat and I could feel hollow cheeks when I touched my face.

In the sitting position, I moved towards the cardboard boxes, pushing myself backward with my good foot and my forearm, dragging my buttocks across the floor. I grabbed one of the boxes by the string that had been tied around it and pulled it down. It landed on the floor with a thud. Then I undid the bowknot and opened it. There were tin cans of corned beef inside, with their respective opening key attached on them.

I opened one of them. I shook the tin up and down and the slab of corned beef came out loose as I grabbed it with the other hand. Then I began to eat it in an almost frenzied fashion. The salty and fatty beef tasted so delicious that I ate it all quickly. Then I washed it down with mineral water. I opened another cardboard box. It contained walnuts and peanuts packed in plastic bags. Having eaten one packet of nuts, I felt full, satisfied. Then, there was nothing else to do but remembering things and thinking things over again, reflecting, wrapped up in deep thoughts, going over the same subject; social contact versus social distance.

I remembered my childhood and adolescence years, and the good times we spent together in that house; Christmas days, New Year Eves, Mother's Day, birthdays, and the party my father made when I finally graduated from the University as a physician. A social and family gathering had always been important to us, because it meant the warmth human contact that happened when people got together.

Aside from exchanging and improving ideas through a common language, social connection also implied a hug, a kiss, holding hands, a looking into somebody's eyes, feeling the skin of a woman. All these seemingly trivial human affairs had always been necessary in the history of mankind, because physical contact had been vital for mental stability and maturity. It made you relax; it slackened the built-up tension and you regained your serenity. Yes, physical contact was balm to the human soul.

Since the first day a human being was born, an infant needed not only the nourishing milk for its body growth but also its mother's nipple, her warm skin, and her loving eyes to look into and find shelter and self-awareness in them, and to be reassured that everything was fine. The bigger the brain a mammal had the more physical contact and protection it needed, and primates had the biggest brain among the mammals, and we were the erect primates endowed with the biggest brain of them all. And now they told us to keep social distance, to stay away from one another, alone, without physical contact, without looking at one another face. They constantly told us to stay at home, hidden from sight.

At the university I had also been taught that without human contact people got anxious and depressed, and anxiety and depression triggered the release of adrenaline in high quantities. High levels of adrenaline were very inflammatory as they weakened the immune system. Thus, the mandatory social distance was a contradiction because it promoted unhealthy mental states and debilitated our protective nature-endowed shield, which was the immune system.

And there I was wrapped up in my loneliness. By government decision and by fate, I had run aground onto the solitary island of my circumstances, which was the cellar of my grandfather house, which I inherited when my parents passed away. I thought of my girlfriend and I wished she were down there, to hug me tightly and feel her warm skin, with her hands on my chest and her breath on my face.

I turned on the radio again. The announcer and commentator were still talking about the disease.

"It seems that the Italian authorities cannot check the propagation of the infection. So far, almost twenty million people have died there so far, most of them in the northern half of the country. Hospitals are collapsing as they had to put up tents out on the streets for the infected ones," the commentator said.

"And what is the Italian government going to do about it? Because twenty million people represent one third of the whole population," the announcer asked.

"Until a vaccine has been developed, they will keep extending the lockdown. I guess, until then entire Italian towns and cities will be almost empty," the commentator said.

"Meanwhile twenty three thousand people died of covid-19 this week-end in Argentina," another announcer said.

'Oh my God! I've got a cousin living in northern Italy!,' I thought. But I was more concerned about my siblings and my girlfriend living in different parts of the city of Tucuman, Argentina.

Tears rolled down my face as the announcers and commentator kept ranting on about the virus and the infection and the importance of staying at home. It was so depressing that I tuned out of it and searched for another station. Switching onto the FM band, I tuned into a radio station that played classical music. Vivaldi concerto in G Major was the soothing elixir for my hurting and gloomy soul. I sighed as I lay down on the floor, sinking into a wistful reverie. Then I felt weary and sleepy. I yawned. Overwhelmed by exhaustion, I spiraled down into fluffy slumber.

When I woke up, I felt as if I had slept for a very long time. I noticed my body skin was dry as I had not broken out in a sweat during sleep. It seemed I did not have fever this time as I saw that the swelling and inflammation had subsided. Although my ankle still hurt when I wiggled my foot, I managed to stand on one foot and jump one step forward, with my side aching at such painful exertion. After trying my physical condition, I sat down back on the floor to have breakfast; corned beef and nuts, washed down with mineral water.

As the days went by, I felt stronger as I tested my body condition. When I say 'days', I mean the time I was awake, since the sunlight did not reach the cellar. Only a yellowish, low-watt electrical bulb that hung over me was the only source of light I had to see around.

Aside from reciting poems by heart, my only entertainment was listening to the radio. According to this mass media source, more than three hundred thousand people had died so far in Tucuman; in other words, one third of its population had been wiped out by the disease. Although I had already resigned myself to the fact that perhaps a brother or some friends, or even my girlfriend, had already died of covid-19, this type of information filled me with anxiety and a sense of total hopelessness as it was repetitive and edited in a way as to deliberately make you sad and break your will to live.

"The president of Argentina said that the peak of the infection has not yet taken place and that we should prepare for the worst next week. Due to the high number of infected people, he ordered another extension of the house confinement. Don't go out. Stay at home," the announcer said.

"Fuck you!" I said, at the announcer, tired of listening to the same trash over and over again. I decided to stop altogether listening to the news, definitely tuning out of that AM radio station as I switched back onto the FM band to listen to some music. I could hardly wait to get out of there.

Finally, the day came when I could stand and walk properly on my two feet as the pain in my side had significantly subsided. I stood for a short while at the stairway landing, looking up into the living-room above. Then I began to climb up the stairs.

When I reached the seventh steps, I jumped over the wide gap, catapulting myself up with my left leg. As I landed on my right foot on the fifth step, I stooped and hung onto the fourth one, feeling a sharp pain in my side. I grimaced as I shook. Then I was able to straighten myself up, regain my balance and walk up out of the underground world where I had lived for I did not know how long.

As soon as I got into the kitchen, the first thing I did was to check my cell phone. There were hundreds of Whatsapps messages that had been sent to me by my siblings, my girlfriend, cousins, uncles, friends, patients, and acquaintances from all over the world. I called my brother and sisters. I was relieved to hear their voices as they were alive and healthy.

"It's great to hear from you, Maximo! Why didn't you answer the messages and the phone calls?" My older brother Juan said.

"I had an accident the day they put us on the lockdown. A stairway step broke as I went down into the cellar. I fell down and broke my leg and a couple of ribs," I said.

"Jesus! That was seven months ago! I thought you had died of covid-19! I tried to go over there and check on you but I was arrested and spent a whole month in prison for violating the quarantine. I'm glad you're alive, little brother! I bet you survived eating the canned corned beef and all the nuts father stored there during the Cold War. He was always afraid of a nuclear winter, too," he said.

"Yeah, that's what I ate! I'm glad that you, your wife, your children and our sisters are alive, too!" I said.

"What are you gonna do now?" He said.

"You know, I haven't taken a shower in seven months. I stink! I'll go to the hospital tomorrow," I said.

"Be careful. There's a rumor that says that hospitals aren't what they used to be," he said.

"I know hospitals. I'm a doctor," I said.

"A lot of things have changed, Maximo. The economy is in deep recession, and there is a shortage of food and people in shanty towns are starving." he said.

As soon as my brother hung up, I called my girlfriend. I was anxious to see her again.

"Don't come over, Maximo. I'm dating my neighbor next door. I'm so sorry, but I thought you had passed away," she said.

I did not keep talking. I did not feel like pleading with her to come back to me, or anything like that. I just thought the whole situation was very unfair to me. With a bitter lump in my throat, I hung up. Then

I went out onto the sidewalk to take a look at the real world. A few neighbors walked up and down the street doing errands. I could not guess who was who, for they all wore surgical masks, just like the ones surgeons wear in an operating room.

I took a deep breath as I opened my mouth wide to let my lungs get filled with fresh air. I looked up at the blue sky, as a gentle breeze blew in my face. A couple of women looked at me from across the street, gawking, with a frown on their foreheads. Inadvertently I drew their attention to myself; I had forgotten that I did not have a T-shirt on, that I was scrawny and I had long hair and a beard, and that I was dirty, and that my human face was naked. I did not know that a nude face had become a taboo, an obscenity.

"Wear a mask, you son of a bitch! You'll spread the disease!" one of them yelled at me.

Showing them the four-letter word finger, I went back inside and headed for the bathroom to take a shower and shave my face clean. The hot water running down my body was so relaxing and soothing that it made me sleepy. I needed a soft bed right away to forget the cold hard floor I slept on for so many nights. It was one O'clock in the afternoon when I lay down on my bed and I fell asleep.

When I woke up four hours later, I still felt tired. So, I went to the kitchen to make some coffee. Then I checked my Whatsapps once again as I began answering all the messages that had been sent by friends and acquaintances when I was down in the cellar. As I sipped the hot, strong coffee, I started to think things over as I put the whole situation in perspective. 'If that pandemic of such infectious disease had been so lethal, with millions of death, as mass media informed, why hadn't it killed anybody I knew?' I thought. Everybody I knew was still alive and in good health.

If it had been so fatal, it would have decimated my Whatsapps and Facebook contacts, including my relatives and close friends. However, not only was every one of them alive, but also the radio announcers, the

TV anchormen, the presidents of nations, the governors of provinces and mayors of every city in Argentina were also alive and politically active. Something was not right as it was hard to put the pieces together to build a mental picture that made sense.

I called the hospital where I worked. Patricia, one of the nurses at the emergency admission, answered the phone.

"Hi, Dr. Garcia! It's nice to hear from you. I thought you had already died!" she said.

"I didn't show up for work because I had an accident. I broke my ankle and I couldn't walk, you know," I said.

"May be you fell because you were already suffering the symptoms of covid-19, which include dizziness. When you show up tomorrow, we're gonna have to take a swab sample from you for a PCR test," she said.

"No, of course not! As I told you, I fell down the stairs because one of the steps broke. It collapsed and I fell through, God-dammed it!" I snarled out.

In my last year at the university, I had been taught the PCR (polymerase chain reaction) test was not reliable, simply because it was not specific for any particular virus. If you tested positive, it only told you that you were infected with an RNA virus. However, it did not specify what kind of RNA virus you were infected with. And there are thousands of RNA viruses that are very important from a pathological point of view, such as rhinoviruses, H1N1, enterovirus, etc. It could also give a positive reaction in the presence of our own genetic material nucleotides, which are molecules that make up an RNA protein strand.

The following morning I went to the hospital where I worked to justify my absence but I also wanted to get an x-ray of my thorax taken and get my ribs checked. On my way, I was stopped three times at different checkpoints, at which there were no nurses or doctors. Set up at every other seven blocks, they were barricades manned by political activists who had been assigned by the leftist government to the task of enforcing the lockdown. Thus, more than sanitary stations that look after disease-afflicted human beings, they truly resembled Cold War-era, Stalinist military checkpoints.

"Where are you going?" one of them inquired, with a bandanna covering his face.

"I'm Dr. Garcia. I'm a clinician who works at Our Lady of the Mercy Hospital," I said, showing him my medical ID.

"Why aren't you wearing a mask? If you're a physician you should know that you have to wear one. It's mandatory by a supreme presidential decree," he said.

"I unintentionally left it at home. I'm in a hurry," I said.

In order for them to let me drive through, I had to make shift with a tissue handkerchief I had in the glove compartment, sticking it to my face with pieces of first aid tape. Having driven for a couple of blocks I stopped at a supermarket to buy a bottle of mineral water and a proper mask from a street vendor peddling on the sidewalk so I could pass through the next checkpoint.

Everybody was wearing a mask, standing in a line, wide apart from one another. I could only see their wide opened eyes, which rolled from side to side in alienation, with a scowl on their forehead. The smile, a symbol of happiness and mental stability, was no longer seen; no more naked faces in sight as the mandatory cloth of censorship had been drawn across to hide humanity.

The mask did not protect people at all from any infectious disease. More than a protective shield, it was a token of tyranny and self-debasement as human beings, who blindly believed what they were being told by mass media, had become the serves of a world-wide sanitary fiefdom, where individual freedom no longer existed. Nature and evolution had endowed us with a much efficient and reliable shield; our immune system.

I arrived at the hospital five minutes later. Dr. Mario Alonso, Laura, and other nurse I did not know were doing the twelve-hour day shift in the emergency receiving room.

"Hi, Laura. Hi, Mario. It's been a long time," I said, slightly bending as I stretched out my forearm to shake their hands, but they refused it, offering me their poignant elbows instead.

"Jesus! I don't have the plague," I said.

"Have you clocked in, yet? Well, don't do it. You have been fired," Dr. Alonso said, gravely.

"Why? I had an accident, for God's sake. I broke my ankle and a couple of ribs. Didn't Patricia tell you?" I said.

"Yes, she did," he said.

"Besides, you're gonna need my professional services. The wards must be full of patients," I said.

"No, they aren't. As a matter of fact, the hospital is almost empty. We only have ten patients with covid-19," Dr. Alonso said.

"There are only ten patients in the whole hospital?" I said.

"Yeah, there're three in the cardiology ward, four in the emergency ward, and three traumatological patients recovering in the clinical ward. Only two patients need respirator, one suffering from a chronic obstructive respiratory disease and the other with mesothelioma," he said.

"So, the whole thing is a God-dammed lie! Just like I'd thought," I said.

"Yes, you're right. I tell you this, you can keep working here if you agree, under a signed contract, to diagnose every patient with covid-19, even if he has a cold or sore throat. You have to talk to the hospital director and he'll have you put back on the payroll. You're gonna be paid more, a lot more," he said.

"I am not sure I can do that, Mario. Let me have a thorax x-ray. I just want to make sure that my ribs have healed and are not protruding into my lung," I said.

Yeah, you can do it. This is a public hospital, you know, but in order to be received in the hospital as a patient, you must accept to be diagnosed with covid-19. You have to sign a form for that, too," Dr. Alonso said.

"No, thanks. I don't wanna be part of this scam. I'd like to tell you this, Mario. The strongest currency is not the US dollar, nor is it a bitcoin. The strongest currency in the history of mankind is honesty. It never gets devalued, because at the end everybody turns to a trustworthy human being to get organized to undertake a project; and the rotten scaffolding will always crumble down under the heavy weight of its own decadence; no matter how powerful it looks," I said, as I turned around and left.

I got into my car and drove aimlessly for a few blocks, drawing up at the park Ninth of July. I got out and walked fifty meters into that green space, stopping at a statue of Juan Bautista Alberdi, set up on a high pedestal in his honor. He was one of the founding fathers of the modern Argentinean State and author of our Constitution, where our individual rights and civil liberties had been established. Crest-fallen, I lay down on the grass as I looked up at him.

The Ninth of July was the name of the park, because it was Argentina's Independence Day. On the July 9, 1816, our founding fathers declared the country's emancipation from Spain and any other foreign powers, meaning that from then on, we would be governed by our own laws, passed by our own representatives. However, the quarantine and its obscure foreign protocols were a major breach of our national sovereignty, and the local politicians had become traitors who had sold themselves to the foreign elite of globalism.

"What are you doing here? You're not supposed to be here," a government activist said, behind a black mask with the image of Che Guevara on it.

"It's my constitutional right to go wherever I please," I said.

"Arrest him and take him to headquarter," he said, to the other thugs.

Having beaten me for a while, they sent me to the nearest police precinct to await a political trial that would have thrown me in prison for several years. Fortunately, the captain in charge of that police unit knew me very well. He was a friend of mine as he had been one of the many patients I had treated successfully in my consulting room.

"It seems that something evil took over this world and have full control of the press, radio, television networks, and the social media on internet," the police officer said, to me.

On the fourth night, after I had recovered a bit from the beating, the police let me and several other detainees escape, under the pretense of a riot and a massive breakout during lunch time.

"When you get out, run as fast as you can. Go to the corner of Moreno St. and Roca boulevard. Somebody will be waiting for you there. He'll have you pass through the checkpoints," he had said, the night before they let me go.

There were two guys waiting for me at that corner. They put me in a Renault Logan trunk and drove for about one and a half hour. When they opened the trunk I found myself in the countryside area at the foot of the local mountain range. They showed me into an old mansion that had been abandoned for decades. It was hidden from view by the thick local vegetation that had grown wild. Nearby there was an old sugar mill lying in dereliction. They sent me food every other ten day.

The police officer was part of resistance group that included citizens from all walks of life. I became part of this freedom fighters movement. We unplug from mass media and got off the internet grid as we set up a ham radio operators network to communicate with one another without being blocked.

Our main objective was to reestablish our independence and civil liberties written in our National Constitution. We needed funds and support, and when we were ready, we rose up in open rebellion.

The Voice

Carlos Benito Camacho

The Voice Carlos B. Camacho

That Sunday I had woken up around ten in the morning. As I opened my eyes and sat up on the edge of my bed, not only did I feel rather dizzy but I also had this strange feeling that something had been lost or taken away from me while I slept. I remember I had had a strong headache the night before. I had tried to watch a movie but I could not focus my attention on that. What started as a maddening, nerve-racking itch deep in my nose had turned into a disturbing pain in my head, especially the front part of it. By the time I had gone to bed, it had become so intense that it felt like a hammer banging on my brain. The pain killer pills I had taken did not work immediately. I had to wait a long while for the headache to slowly begin to ebb away as I lay in bed. It was as if the pillow began to soften from the piece of hard rock it felt it was as I started to relax. Then I finally went to sleep.

Sitting on the edge of my bed, I attempted to start up my awareness and focus it on something; but my mind was still hazy as I tried to figure out what I should do next, but I did not know what. It was weird. It was though I had lost my chronological bearings. I finally got up and walked a couple of steps towards the bathroom to take a cold shower to fully wake myself up and dispel my confusion, but I stopped halfway, not being sure if that was the right thing to do, looking around the room in confusion. The window was wide open and the morning sunlight slantingly fell into my room. The walls were behung with pictures of relatives and me wearing different types of army uniforms.

A strong breeze began to blow from the south. As I looked out at the distant oncoming clouds, I suddenly heard a voice that came out of nowhere. It assertively talked to me, as if instructing me what to do next. It was the first time I heard it.

"Get dressed, go get your gun from the closet, grab your backpack and fill it with food and ammunition," the voice said.

"Who are you?!" I shouted, startled at the intruding voice.

"Hurry up! You don't have much time, for you are going to have to run for your life," the voice said, overriding my question. "Hurry up, hurry up!" it said, piercing my ears and reverberating inside me.

As the black clouds came over and cloaked the morning sun, it suddenly dawned on me that I had read a piece of foreboding information the week before. I could not remember exactly what type of information it was, but I had the feeling it was certainly ominous. My head hurt when I tried to remember the details. Then, with a sense of impending evil, I did as the voice had said. I filled my backpack with food and cartridges and took my old, Ithaca 37, 12-gauge shotgun that I kept in the closet.

As I came out onto the front porch, strange lightning broke loose from the black clouds above and hit the distant ground. They were not ordinary, jagged bolts of lightning that we usually see streaking across the sky during a summer storm but smooth, tubular ones, like beams of violet light vertically projecting to earth from those strange clouds.

"Check on it," the voice whispered in my ear.

I went upstairs, grabbed the telescope and came out onto the balcony to take a better look. Each time a pipe of lightning struck the ground, a bipedal, man-like creature popped into view. It smelled like sulfur in the air, as if the devil himself were nearby.

"Run!" the voice said.

I went down and got into the car as fast as I could but I could not get it to start. The ignition was dead. I got out and began to run towards the town to warn my friends who lived there.

The town was about half a mile in a straight line from my house. Running fast, I cut across the grassy plain. One of the horrible, horned creatures was about to overtake me.

"Watch out, watch out! It's behind you!" the voice warned me.

I spun around fast and blew it to pieces as I fell backwards in the tall grass.

"On your right!" the voice shouted at me as I tried to rise from the ground.

I swept the barrel of the gun ninety degrees to my right and shot again, making a big gaping hole in the middle of the second creature. It dripped slimy bluish blood as it fell lifeless. Strange vapors rose up from the grass where it fell.

I got up and kept running wild across the cattle-strewn plain. As I ran, I saw dismembered dead cows lying around, jumping over them as I went. Then I waded through a creek that flowed across a corn field and disappeared into the forest.

The tall, leafy trees muffled out the thunderous noises produced by the ionized, steamy obscurity in the sky. Concealed from view, I felt protected in the cozy silence of the thick forest. However, I kept on running, crashing through the undergrowth as I went. I soon became exhausted and my shirt got wet with sticky sweat. I felt my tongue dry as I breathed heavily through gaping mouth. Slimy saliva trickled down my chin. I stopped to get my breath back as I came out into a clearing in the woods.

I stooped, with my hands resting on my knees, panting. I thought I heard someone walking or maybe I felt the presence of someone in the deep shade of the forest. I looked around, but I saw no one, nothing. In front of me, there was a small stream flowing across the woods. It was swift-running water that gurgled over its stony bed. Then I threw myself down on the ground to quench my thirst.

As I drank the cool, crystal-clear water, the voice whispered, "look up."

I raised my head from the water and I saw a tall man standing right in front of me on the other side of the clearing. His image was somewhat blurred, misty-like. He was dressed in medieval warrior outfit, but he looked more like a Viking than a knight in armor, and instead of a sword, he carried a big, steel hammer.

"I am the voice. Don't be afraid of the storm now. The dark clouds and the beastly ghosts can no longer reach you here," he said solemnly.

"You? But I heard you before at my house and in the cornfield and I didn't see you," I said. "It was just a voice that sounded in my head," I added.

"Remember the information," he said.

After a hard mental exertion, I was finally able to retrieve the information from some murky corner of my mind. It had been sent to my wife's e-mail address the week before. She had gone out to do an errand, inadvertently leaving her e-mail box open.

I had been operated on for schizophrenia on a pseudo diagnose. Hippocampal and frontal nerve fibers had been cut in my brain, isolating some areas of my cerebral cortex from one another.

"Who ordered the operation," I asked.

"The former government did. They are the same men that let the aliens in. You knew too much and the lobbyists decided that you should be rendered mentally disabled," he said.

"I don't know what I should do now. I feel as if I lack the will power to act on my own," I said.

"Don't worry. I'll be the fortress and the booster behind your every act. Go to town now and get ready to fight, for the strife is going to be long. The black clouds have dissipated but the beastly ghosts they bore are already taking human forms. I'll always be whispering guiding words to you from the right side of your brain," he said, as he vanished in midair.

Disturbances

Carlos B. Camacho

Disturbances Carlos B. Camacho

Philippe Belmond had moved into a big, stately house in the countryside, in the rural area around the town of Lules, Tucuman, in the northwest of Argentina. It was his newly acquired property. He had discovered it through an ad he had read in the local newspaper just after he had arrived in the capital of that province. As soon as he saw it, he made up his mind to buy it right away, for it was a French, cottage-style villa, which reminded him of the country houses around Dijon, in the French Burgundy, where he was born and grew up. It was made of limestone, had five bedrooms, and its gabled roof was covered with overlapping, clay, barrel tiles. It had been built at the beginning of the 20th century by a rich man who owned a sugar mill that now lay derelict about one hundred and fifty yards away.

The house was also in bad condition when he bought it, for one of its rooms had been gutted by fire, which had blackened the walls, leaving a big, gaping hole in its roof. Although he got it repaired and painted on the inside, on the outside, the mossy stone walls and the mildewed roof tiles gave the house an air of mystery mixed with ghastliness. That was the impression the local folks got whenever they saw it, but it struck him as romantic, as the villa sat in a lush, subtropical environment. It was surrounded by sugar cane fields and lemon groves, with the jungle-covered Aconquija Mountain range's foothills in the background. A small river ran between two distant ridges out onto the plain, flowing by five hundred yards away from the house. There was a seven-month period of rainy season, with the sugar cane harvest taking place during the year dry spell, when all the sugar mills in the small province of Tucuman began spouting out plumes of black smoke into the air through long, black stacks, polluting the atmosphere, except for the one that stood idle nearby. But the air was clean in the summer time, during which there were spells of rains and sunshine.

Philippe was a former member of the French communist party. He was an idealist, who always took a biased stand on political and social issues as he saw the world around him through jaundiced eyes, taking part in the French civil unrest of May 1968 against Charles de Gaulle's government as he supported and advocated any leftist guerrilla movement around the world no matter how violent they were. As a byproduct of the Cold War years, he acted spontaneously by unbridled reaction to the events impinging upon him, and not by reflective, rational, crystal-clear thinking. His mind was not anchored to reality, where there were the real human beings, but to the idealistic world of socialist authors' works he had read. And Philippe was idealist because he had grown up in the isolated world of the rich man's son.

Thus, when he inherited a small fortune upon his father death in 1983, he decided to travel down to South America to settle there and invest his money in Argentina, the home country of tango, which was the favorite music played and danced in the French upper class ballrooms, and of Che-Guevara, the renown guerrilla commander. He had read a lot about this South American country, about Juan Domingo Peron and Evita, the military coups, and the leftist insurgency. The year he moved down to Argentina, the country held its first general elections after six and half year of military government.

Thus, the prospect of taking up residence in that country ideally looked good, for an idealist. He preferred to settle in the northwest of Argentina, since its subtropical landscape, with the sugar cane fields and the jungle-covered ridges in the West, resembled Cuba, which was the first country where a communist revolution had succeeded in the Western Hemisphere, radiating ideological disturbances that reached university classrooms and libraries throughout Latin America.

The day he had moved into the house he went out for a walk, to explore and get to know the surrounding area and the few neighbors who lived in shacks sparsely sitting along the dirt road. It was sunny and warm. He was wearing a pair of khaki shorts, a black T-shirt, with a picture of Che-Guevara on it, and a white cap. He walked past the abandoned sugar mill, in the direction of the river. As he went, a flock of green parrots flew up from a mulberry tree, squawking loud as they fluttered towards the ravine. Amid the barking of scrawny mongrel dogs, he stopped in front of a humble home and introduced himself to an old man that sat on a low, wooden stool as he fed corn to the chickens.

"Good afternoon! My name is Philippe. I'm your new neighbor. I've just moved into that big house over there," he said, with a strong French accent, pointing to the villa.

"Are you going to live there?" uttered the old man, doddering a little bit, rolling his eyes from side to side. Then, he closed them for a couple of seconds and carried on feeding the chickens.

Philippe continued to walk along the narrow road. Having crossed a small bridge spanning the river, he met a peasant that came from the opposite direction, at a point where there were nine little crosses by the wayside.

"Hello! How are you? I'm Philippe, from France," he introduced himself.

"Good afternoon, Sir," the peasant greeted, respectfully, taking off his felt hat.

"What do these crosses mean? Are they marking the site of a massive execution? I mean, freedom fighters murdered by the national army during the last military regime?" Philippe inquired.

"No, Sir. The little crosses mark the site of a massive execution of nine peasants, murdered by the outsiders, the ERP communist guerrillas, in 1975, during the democratic government before the military coup. They were accused by the terrorists of giving information on their presence in the area to the Argentinean Army" he said. Then he asked, "are you living in that big stone house over there?"

"Yes, I'm your new neighbor. I'm going to buy land and perhaps reopen the sugar mill," Philippe said.

"You're going to open a business, Sir, with that T-shirt?" the humble peasant said. He looked at Philippe, then at the villa in the distance, then at the Che-Guevara picture in his T-shirt. A few seconds went by when all of a sudden, he broke into a loud guffaw that sounded like the bray of a donkey, looking up at the sky with wide open mouth, showing gaps in between his rotten teeth as he continued his way.

"What's wrong with this guy," Philippe muttered in French and kept on walking in the opposite direction.

The sugar cane harvest had not begun yet, so the air was still clean, except for a light haze of wood smoke that drifted from a domed, adobe oven sitting next to a thatch-roofed house. Philippe breathed in the air and noticed that it also smelled of fresh, home-made bread, making him even hungrier. He had not had lunch; too busy helping the moving van guys unload the furniture and distribute the different pieces around the house.

He stopped in front of the modest house, with the oven. Nobody was around, only a few clucking chickens in the front yard and a couple of grunting pigs in the sty.

"Is there anybody home!" he said, as he whistled and clapped his hands to draw the attention of the home dwellers. Finally, a wizened, old woman showed up, coming around the side of the shack from the backyard.

"What do you want, Mr?" she said, doddering.

"Good afternoon, Madam. I'm your new neighbor. I was passing by and I saw the oven there, and I was wondering if you, perhaps, could sell me some home-made bread.

"Yes, I figure I can sell some bread to you. I have a batch in the oven right now, and I was about to get it out," she said.

As the lady went over to get the bread out, Philippe looked around and noticed an old, partly-burned, Chevrolet 400 Special car that was parked beside the house. It was abandoned, rusted, and seemed to have been riddled with bullets.

The old woman came over with two loaves of hot, crusty bread wrapped up in a worn kitchen towel. "That'll be 15 pesos, with the towel included" she said.

"What happened to that car? Did the Argentinean Army assassinate someone in there?" he asked.

"No, Mr., some leftist terrorists did that. They killed the driver and then kidnapped the businessman who was in the back seat. We never heard of him ever since; missing, probably executed in the jungle. The car came handy, though. We use it as a hen brooding house.

On the way back home, Philippe stopped on the bridge for a while, looking down into the flowing waters of Lules River, thinking things over, rummaging the deep recesses of his mind as he looked for a philosophical answer. Wearing the Che-Guevara T-shirt, he felt like an idiot. After six years of military regime, the local folks did not act the way he had expected them to act and they did not say the things he had expected them to say. "They don't look like the kind of people who suffered oppression," he thought.

That evening he had a couple of fried eggs, with home-made bread and a piece of cheese for desert. The sun had just set behind the mountains in the west. He gazed out of the kitchen window as he ate. The wild grass, the sugar canes, and the tree trunks were being engulfed by darkness that seemed to be alive, exuding out of the earth like an evil thing that crawled up upon everything on its surface. A neighbor's radio blared out cheap, strident music in the distance for a while; then it went out altogether.

As silence slowly pervaded the new reality around him, he began to feel exhausted, but also lonely. He never got married and did not have children, perhaps out of selfishness. He did fall in love once, though, with a Vietnamese girl who had gotten killed in the French-Indochina War, during his residence in Southeast Asia in support of the communist party against the French colonial government. He missed her very much as she had left a deep void inside him. It was a tragic event in his life. Coming to Argentina was perhaps an escape. But that had been a bitter niche in his past; Argentina was his present circumstances then. The strange barking of a fox in the distance stopped his train of thoughts as he wondered what on earth that was. But it had been a long day. He yawned and felt like going to bed.

He went upstairs, opened wide the window to air the house, then went into the bathroom to take a shower. When he came out, a black bat flew in and perched upside down on one of the roof rafters above a Karl Marx bust standing near a chest of drawers. With its prehensile feet, it tightly clutched a big rusted nail that protruded from the beam wood as it screeched, flashing its tiny, dagger-shaped teeth. It was a South American, hematophagous species of bat. Astonished at the sight, he stood frozen in place, staring up at the ceiling.

"A bloodsucking bat! What a grotesque version of Poe's Raven!" he thought. "You, thing of evil, carrier of rabies, go back to the river shore to suck somebody else's Plutonian blood!" he yelled, whipping at the creature with his bath towel.

But the bat was out of reach of the towel and remained hanging adamantly upside down from its perching support on the rafter. The bat screeched one more time and swooped down on him at his neck. Philippe screamed, then yelled and cursed as he tried to desperately brush it off of him. The bat could not bite his neck but it tore open his skin with its razor-sharp teeth as it was swept away by Philippe's hand.

Like a high-tech fighter aircraft, the bat maneuvered around his waist, then it soared up to its perch on the rafter, screeching and moving its ears. The little monster partially opened its small wings and plummeted down on him again, going straight to his crotch. However, this time Philippe was ready and whacked it down against the floor with a book he had just grabbed from the night table, trampling on it several times with the heel of his foot until it got squashed up flat, with guts and blood spurting out of it.

"Don't ever dream you're gonna suck my dick, you bloodsucking faggot!" he muttered, as he threw the dead bat out of the window, closing the sash fast, then checking every nook and cranny in the bedroom for any other horrendous, exotic creature that might have sneaked into the house while he was taking the shower.

Exhausted, he was finally able to turn in. He switched off the lamp on the night table, lying in bed on the alert for any further air attack. Then, the state of alertness began to subside as he sank into a reverie, recalling his past; thinking of his former wife, his native town and his youth years; although he had traveled a lot and been away from his mother country only a couple of weeks, he already missed his relatives and friends. Settling in the northwest of Argentina was a big decision he had made in his life.

Suddenly, he noticed that it was so quiet that his ears rang. After a short while, he started to relax. Then sleep came over slowly, in fluffy waves that crept up every muscle in his body and leaked into his brain, paralyzing any action. However, at the gates of unconsciousness he could still hear something, or thought he could hear something; whispering voices that came from downstairs; "please, help me, help me, come on, help me," but another wave of slumber took over his brain as he felt like sliding into a hole in the bed, then falling down into a deep, dark well.

As he fell, he saw blurred human faces distorted by pain or some kind of suffering in the depths of the well. Then, he began to feel stifled; he needed air. He tried to breathe, but the air would not go into his lungs. Just before he reached the bottom, he was stopped dead by a noose that closed in tightly around his neck. Flailing his arms in desperation, he woke up, covered in sweat. As he regained consciousness, Philippe desperately fumbled about for the switch of the bedside table lamp. Struggling to get some air, he managed to turn on the light as he jumped out of bed, still feeling the snare around his neck.

He urgently tried to get it off, clawing at his neck with his fingers as he stood in front of the mirror to see what was strangling him. In the dim light of the bedside table lamp, he fleetingly saw a ghastly, red face, with swollen, bulging eyes, like the face of a man being hanged on the gallows. A deep, low-pitched, rasping scream tore out of his lungs as he gasped in horror. But then, he began to see his own normal face again in the mirror, groping clumsily his head to reassure himself that it was his. Panting and rolling his eyes from side to side, he stooped, resting his hands on his knees.

"Oh my God! Was it a horrible nightmare? Or was it real?" he wondered, looking down at the floor. He was still breathing heavily and his mouth was as dry as sandpaper.

As he stood up and made for the bathroom to drink a glass of water, he caught a fleeting glimpse of a child silhouette, or perhaps a dwarf, that stood on the first step of the stairway that led down to the kitchen and the dining-room. The blurred figure scampered down quickly into the gloom of the stairway. Apprehensively, Philippe slowly went down the stairs, with his heartbeat accelerating again.

As soon as he got into the kitchen, he heard a whispering voice of a woman asking for help. Her plea reverberated in his head. He went up the stairs back into his bedroom, bringing his hands to his ears. He got back in bed, but this time he did not go back to sleep. He lay wide awake, staring at the ceiling, trying to find a logical explanation, with his heart rate dangerously increasing. He came to the conclusion that it was just a nightmare, attributing the vision and hearing perceptions to stress and mental fatigue as a result of adapting to a new cultural environment.

However, these sleep disturbances went on for several more nights, in which the arrhythmia, shortness of breath and chest pain increased, with his mental state worsening. So, one morning, he drove down to the city to see a doctor, who prescribed him atenolol, clonazepam, and some rest.

"Don't worry, Mr Belmond. It's just exhaustion and stress; just take it easy and relax," the heart specialist said.

Philippe decided to temporarily stop the revamping and restart of the old dilapidated sugar mill he had just bought, and to take a break. He resolved to try to forget business for a while, and his past. He hired a live-in, young maid to cook and do the house cleaning, and provide him with some, warm company.

With a female companion in the villa, the disturbances seemed to have abated as the stress that afflicted him slackened a little. However, one evening, as he was about to finish mowing the back yard grass, he heard a scream coming out of the living-room. Then, he saw the maid run out of the house.

"Oh, my God! This place is haunted! I'm not coming back!" she said, distraught, as she panted heavily.

"What happened?" he said.

"I heard voices and groans; then I saw human shadows that moved about in the house. And I feel this tightness in my chest. I can hardly breathe," said the maid, as she left.

The following day, a peasant that passed by found Philippe's body lying, fatally injured, on the steel disks of the old plow that lay on the front garden. It looked as though the French man had jumped out of the bedroom window in desperation, escaping from some horrible nightmare. His wide opened eyes and distorted face expressed total horror.

Long before Philippe Belmond had traveled to Argentina, the house had been seized by the federal authorities during the guerrilla war years upon the mysterious disappearance of the whole family that once lived in there. It was later sold at a public auction by the government. Since Philippe was its third resident to die in there under strange and tragic circumstances, with the villa being acquired three times by new owners, the local police initiated a thorough investigation to determine the cause of their death and find the culprit, if there was one.

Having interrogated several rural, senior citizens inhabiting the countryside area, the police obtained a warrant from a judge to carry out a thorough search of the villa and its surrounding grounds. According to one of the witnesses' testimony, a gang of "construction workers" were the last persons seen come out of the house before the original owner's family was reported missing, loading shovels and pick axes onto a Ford pick-up truck, speeding away out of sight. That had been about eight or nine years before, when the Argentinean Army had just begun a heavy military operation against the Marxist guerrilla forces that operated in the Northwest of Argentina.

The police officers first searched the first floor. Then they went down to the ground level, moving furniture about. Then, remembering the witness saying that he had seen the "construction workers" loading pick-axes and shovels, a Sergeant started knocking about the floor with a hammer. When the sound of the hammer striking the tiled ground of the house turned hollow, he ordered his men to break the floor and dig in there.

Under the living-room floor, which had been entirely retiled by the runaway gang, there was a large hole containing the rotten corpses of the missing family; husband, wife, and three children, who had all been shot in the head, with their hands tied behind them. However, there was another corpse in the house pit; it was an adult, male human that apparently had been choked to death with a wire garrote tightly wrapped around what remained of his neck. This male corpse would be identified several weeks later by police coroners thanks to a broad-band silver ring they found on one of his fingers. The ring's inner surface bore the victim's full name and his wife's carved in tiny capital letters.

The man that had been strangled with the garrote was an Argentinean Army's undercover agent. The owner and his family had been kept in captivity in their own house by the Marxist terrorists for a month before being executed. The pit dug out in the living-room area was a classic "people's jail"; a clandestine detention center, in which these communist insurgent groups used to keep businessmen, labor union leaders, and military personnel they kidnapped during the dirty war years.